"Yes or no, Alesha." His expression was unreadable, his eyes dark and unwavering as they regarded her.

It had to be yes. "I have no choice but to agree, subject to certain conditions."

There was a strength apparent in her demeanor, a determination he could only admire given she'd taken a king-sized hit about the true state of her father's corporation.

"Name them." His voice held a silkiness she chose to ignore.

"I retain my position in Karsouli."

Loukas inclined his head in agreement. "Naturally."

Now for the cruncher. "A separate suite of rooms in whatever home we share."

His gaze narrowed. "Your reason being?"

"A personal preference."

He regarded her in silence for several timeless seconds. "The same bedroom, separate beds." He waited a beat. "Until you feel comfortable sharing mine."

All about the author...
Helen Bianchin

HELEN BIANCHIN grew up in New Zealand, an only child possessed by a vivid imagination and a love for reading. After four years of legal secretarial work, Helen embarked on a working holiday in Australia where she met her Italian-born husband, a tobacco sharefarmer in far north Queensland. His command of English was pitiful, and her command of Italian was nil. Fun? Oh yes! So, too, was being flung into cooking for workers immediately after marriage, stringing tobacco and living in primitive conditions.

It was a few years later when Helen, her husband and their daughter returned to New Zealand, settled in Auckland and added two sons to their family. Encouraged by friends to recount anecdotes of her years as a tobacco sharefarmer's wife living in an Italian community, Helen began setting words on paper and her first novel was published in 1975.

Creating interesting characters and telling their stories remain as passionate a challenge for Helen now as it did in the beginning of her writing career.

Spending time with family, reading and watching movies are high on Helen's list of pleasures. An animal lover, Helen says her maltese terrier and two Birman cats regard her study as much theirs as hers.

Helen Bianchin

THE ANDREOU MARRIAGE ARRANGEMENT

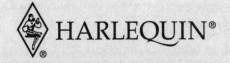

HARLEQUIN®

TORONTO • NEW YORK • LONDON
AMSTERDAM • PARIS • SYDNEY • HAMBURG
STOCKHOLM • ATHENS • TOKYO • MILAN • MADRID
PRAGUE • WARSAW • BUDAPEST • AUCKLAND

Recycling programs
for this product may
not exist in your area.

ISBN-13: 978-0-373-23705-0

THE ANDREOU MARRIAGE ARRANGEMENT

First North American Publication 2010.

Printed in U.S.A.

THE ANDREOU MARRIAGE ARRANGEMENT

CHAPTER ONE

ALESHA sat in stunned silence as the lawyer finished reading her late father's will.

Surprise didn't even begin to cut it.

What had Dimitri Karsouli been *thinking* in selling a twenty-five-per-cent share in the Karsouli Corporation to Loukas Andreou?

Worse…gifting Loukas a further twenty-five-per-cent share. Representing several hundred million dollars on today's market.

Subject to marriage.

The breath caught in her throat as realization hit. Dear heaven. Her father had *bought* her a husband?

It was beyond comprehension.

Yet she was all too aware how her father's mind worked; it didn't take much to do the maths.

A year ago Alesha's disastrous short-lived marriage had formally ended in divorce from a man who had professed to love her…only for her to discover to her cost that Seth Armitage's main goal had been a stake in her father's fortune and a free ride on the gravy train. It had devastated her and angered her father…more than she had known.

Dimitri, out of a sense of parental devotion, had clearly conspired to arrange what he perceived to be a fail-safe liaison for his daughter via marriage to a man who had his total approval. A man of integrity, trust, possessed of astute business nous, and a worthy companion.

Loukas Andreou, the inflexible omnipotent head of the Athens branch of the Andreou Corporation, whose financial interests included shipping and considerable ancillary assets worldwide.

Loukas, whose father Constantine had been Dimitri's lifelong friend and associate…a man whose powerful image sprang so readily to Alesha's mind, it was almost as if his presence became a tangible entity in the room.

In his late thirties, attractive, if one admired masculine warrior features, with the height, breadth of shoulder and facial bone structure that comprised angles and planes. Loukas had brilliant dark eyes and a mouth that promised much.

Sophisticated apparel did little to diminish an innate ruthlessness resting beneath the surface of his control.

It was utterly devastating for Alesha to even begin to imagine what had possessed Dimitri to revise his will to include a clause stipulating his bequest of the remaining fifty-per-cent share in the Karsouli Corporation to his only child, Alesha Eleni Karsouli. This bequest was conditional on a marriage taking place to Loukas Andreou within a month of Dimitri's demise, thus ensuring a one-hundred-per-cent joint *family* ownership, thereby securing the corporation and ensuring it would continue into another generation.

'A court of law could rule the marriage stipulation as invalid,' Alesha voiced.

The lawyer regarded her thoughtfully. 'While there would be a degree of sympathy regarding that specific clause, your father's instructions were very clearly defined. I counselled him to reconsider, but he was adamant that clause should stand.'

Alesha stifled a startled curse beneath her breath.

Dimitri had known how much Karsouli meant to her, how she'd lived and breathed it for as long as she could remember. Absorbing every aspect, studying for degrees at university to ensure she acquired the relevant knowledge, the edge... aware the word *nepotism* didn't exist in her father's vocabulary.

He knew too the pride she'd taken in working her way from the ground up to her current position of authority.

It had been a foregone conclusion his only child would assume control upon Dimitri's demise.

And he had, Alesha conceded, gifted her that…with strings attached. Conditions aimed to protect Karsouli, and her. Especially *her*.

To attempt to force her into a marriage she didn't want was the ultimate manipulative act, and in that moment she could almost hate him for it.

Two days ago she'd weathered the funeral service at the chapel. Walked behind the hearse to the grave site. Stood in silent despair and grieved as the ritual played out.

Aware of Loukas Andreou's presence…imagining he'd flown in from Athens to attend Dimitri's funeral as a mark of respect. And totally unaware of any subterfuge.

She could walk away; ignore the marriage clause, resign from the Karsouli Corporation and seek a position in a rival firm.

Except she was a Karsouli, born and bred, legally reverting to her maiden name after her failed marriage. Hadn't her father groomed her to rise to her current position? Conditioning her to believe it didn't matter she was female; women in the twenty-first century held positions of power, and he'd given her no reason to suppose otherwise.

Dimitri Karsouli had ruled his life and his business interests with an iron fist in a velvet glove, earning him a corporation now worth a fortune.

His father before him had come from humble beginnings in Athens, and, fostering an idea presented to the right person at the right time, initiated the founding office in Athens of the Karsouli Corporation. Dimitri, his only son, had followed in hallowed footsteps, living and breathing the business and injecting it with new ideas, broadening its scope and extending it onto a global market.

Dimitri had married and moved to Sydney and had sought to have his own son continue, except his marriage had gifted him a daughter, born in difficult circumstances that had rendered his wife unable to produce another child.

A beloved daughter, Alesha, who had become her father's pride and joy, especially when she proved she'd inherited his business acumen and sharp mind.

Privately educated and exclusively schooled, Alesha had graduated from university with honours in a business degree, and had entered

Karsouli in a lowly position, rising in the ranks through hard work and dedication.

Her one error in judgement had been to marry in haste, against her father's wishes, a man who, while playing a part to perfection during their brief courtship, had revealed his true persona within hours of leaving the wedding reception.

A painful time, when divorce and a handsome pay-out had been the only option. Especially so, as it was compounded by her mother's losing battle with a virulent form of cancer.

Alesha's adamant refusal to consider marriage at any future stage became a bone of contention between father and daughter. Now, by a conditional clause in his will, Dimitri was bent on manipulating her into matrimony with a man of whom he approved. A man of Greek descent. Someone who had his utmost trust…to take the reins of Karsouli and lead his daughter into the marriage bed.

Dimitri had to be smiling in his grave, assured Alesha would never concede to losing what she loved most in life…the family firm.

In that respect she'd inherited her father's genes. His bloodline was so strong, the desire to achieve, to succeed, to prove her worth beyond doubt, irrespective of gender.

'This…*scheme* has Loukas Andreou's approval?'

The lawyer spread his hands in a telling gesture. 'I understand he has indicated his consent.'

'It's outrageous,' Alesha uttered with considerable heat. '*Impossible*,' she added for good measure. 'I don't want to marry *anyone*.'

Loukas Andreou had been welcomed into her parents' home on the few occasions he'd visited Sydney. She'd dined in his company, and met up with him in Athens on the occasional trip to Greece with her parents. Combining business with pleasure…or so she'd thought at the time.

Now, she wasn't so sure. Even *then*, had Dimitri sown the seeds of a possible future marriage?

Loukas Andreou. The man was a force to be reckoned with in the business arena…and the bedroom, if rumour had any basis in fact.

Old money. His great-grandfather, so the Andreou biographical details depicted on record revealed, had made his fortune in shipping. A fortune added to by each succeeding generation.

The Andreou consortium owned two Greek Islands, property, residences in most European cities, and there was the private cruiser, the Lear jet, the expensive cars…the women.

The media followed and tabled Loukas' every move, embellishing the smallest fact with gossip.

Tall, well-built frame, dark hair, ruggedly attractive facial features…he unsettled her. Almost as if he saw far more than she wanted anyone to see.

There were some secrets she'd buried so deep, no one would uncover them. Ever.

'How long has Loukas been aware of the contents of my father's will?'

'It's something you'll have to ask him.'

She would…at the first opportunity!

Alesha glimpsed the faint lift in the lawyer's brow.

'You have two clear options,' he cautioned quietly. 'Agree to the marriage…or disagree. I strongly advise you not to make a decision until you've spoken with Loukas Andreou.'

She stood and indicated the consultation had reached a conclusion. The lawyer accompanied her into the lobby and pressed the call button to summon a lift.

Alesha gritted her teeth together in a need to prevent the urge to scream as the lift transported her to ground. *Why* had her father conspired to do what he had?

Except she knew precisely why.

Hadn't Dimitri's own marriage to her mother been deemed a satisfactory liaison benefitting both families?

Love? If it happened, well and good. If it didn't, affection, *family* was enough to make a contented life.

Surprisingly, her parents had shared a good marriage. A little volatile at times, she reflected, remembering Dimitri's voice raised in anger over some relatively minor conflict with her mother. A woman who'd stood her own ground and given back as much in kind. Had they shared a grand passion? Perhaps. Great affection, certainly.

Alesha had wanted the grand passion, the love generated by two souls in perfect accord. She'd thought she'd found it with Seth Armitage…only to discover he'd very cleverly played a cruel game, and her marriage was nothing more than a travesty. One she escaped from almost as soon as the ink had dried on their marriage certificate.

Dimitri, to give him his due, hadn't vented with *I told you so*. He'd been supportive, caring.

Yet it hurt unbearably that behind the scenes he'd been conspiring to cement her future and the future of Karsouli. Worse, somehow, was Loukas Andreou's complicity.

To think she'd accepted his condolences, shared his presence during the funeral service, suffered his silent watchfulness…and he *knew*.

Dear Lord in heaven.

Was she the only one who'd been in ignorance?

At this very moment, was Loukas Andreou already putting plans in motion to assume prime position within Karsouli?

Or had he already done that, skilfully lining everything up to ensure any hiccups would be only minor? And if he had, how could she have missed *seeing* it? Surely there should have been something, even subtle, that would have alerted her attention?

Yet even on brief reflection, she failed to pinpoint any one thing.

The Sydney skyline was slightly hazy in the prelude to evening dusk, the harbour assuming a darker hue as ferries left a white churning tail as they transported some of the city's workers to the northern suburb of Manly. Her apartment formed part of a large old double-storeyed home in fashionable Double Bay, whose interior had been completely restructured into four self-contained two-bedroom apartments. Modern state-of-the-art appliances blended beautifully with the deliberate styling of the previous century.

It had given Alesha immense pleasure to add furnishings to complement the era…large comfortable sofas, antique furniture, exquisite lamps and beautiful Oriental rugs, large squares and runners providing an attractive foil for the stained wooden floors.

Home, for the past two years. *Hers*, alone.

Something completely different from the modern house gifted to her on her wedding day. A home she'd legally tussled over with Seth, along with his claim for a half share, together with a half share of the assets she'd brought to the marriage.

A slight shudder scudded down the length of her spine as she garaged her car.

Seth, the handsome charmer who'd played so skilfully into her hands…and who, once vows legalized their union, with his ring on her finger, had dropped the pretence he'd so carefully fostered.

Even now with hindsight, she had trouble relating the charmer to the hard, calculating monster he became.

It's gone, done and dusted, Alesha dismissed as she entered the spacious foyer and trod the stairs to her apartment.

She was whole again, mentally and physically. Dating wasn't on her agenda…hadn't been since she'd walked out on her marriage. She had friends…a trusted few whose company she valued.

Life, until her father's death a week ago, had become settled, predictable, *comfortable*.

Now it was about to take a backwards flip into

the uncertain, and instinct warned she'd need all her wits to cope with whatever lay ahead.

Marriage to Loukas Andreou?

If it happened, it would be on *her* terms.

She entered the apartment, ditched her bag, laptop, toed off her stilettos, then padded into the kitchen and filched chilled water from the refrigerator.

A leisurely shower, then she'd fix dinner…and plan her strategy.

Conditions, she elaborated as she shed her tailored suit, stripped to the skin and walked naked into the en suite.

A paper marriage; separate bedrooms; separate private lives. They'd work together in harmony; confer and co-ordinate their social diaries in order to entertain and grace the requisite social functions.

Alesha adjusted the water dial and stepped beneath the generous spray, collected delicately scented gardenia soap and attempted to match her marriage strategy to the man Dimitri had deliberately selected as her *second* husband.

'Hell's teeth,' she muttered with unaccustomed ire. She didn't *want* a husband!

On the occasions she'd shared Loukas' company, he'd been attentive, an interesting conversationalist, knowledgeable, intelligent, focused.

Sexy, a silent imp added, in a leashed, almost primitive manner that hinted at much and promised more.

Alesha closed her eyes, then slowly opened them again.

Where had that come from?

Oh, for heaven's sake, admit it. There had been a time when she'd wondered what it would be like to have his mouth close over her own, and savour, taste…persuade. To lean in against his body and absorb his strength, and discover…*what*? Attraction, *more*?

She'd caught a sense of it, become fascinated by him, even curious…aware he met with her parents' approval. A man of independent wealth and substance. Attentive, watchful, almost *waiting*, she reflected. For what? For her to make the first move?

Except she hadn't. Instinctively aware if she did, there would be no going back.

Perhaps, she allowed in retrospect, Dimitri had begun to hope, to plan…even then.

Except Seth had already been on the scene, sweeping her off her feet with glib words and false promises. Words and promises she had believed to be genuine, in spite of her parents' caution.

From beautiful to battered bride in the space of

a heartbeat…okay, *weeks*, Alesha corrected grimly as she closed the water dial, caught up a towel and wrapped it round her slender curves.

Leading, she admitted, to the most painful months of her life as she had weathered the aftermath, regained her self-respect…*dammit*, her very identity.

Together with a resolve never to allow anyone to get close enough to earn her personal trust again. A fact she'd set down in stone, with a frozen heart and a cool, determined brain.

The evening stretched ahead, and one she'd choose to fill after a light meal with a few hours spent on her laptop, catch the late news on television…then bed.

It seemed like a plan, albeit a familiar one as she swept the length of her hair into a careless knot, donned underwear before adding comfortable jeans and a singlet top.

The message light was blinking on her answering machine as she entered the kitchen, and she crossed to the servery, took up a pen, pulled the message pad forward and pressed the *play* button.

"Alesha. Loukas Andreou." His voice was deep, husky, with a slight accented inflection that curled round her nerve-ends and tugged a little. It wasn't a feeling she coveted, and she drew in a calming breath as she noted down the number he recited. "Call me."

A soft curse emerged from her lips, and she rolled her eyes in silent self-castigation. He wasn't wasting any time.

So make the call. The sooner she dealt with him, the better.

He picked up on the third ring. 'Andreou.'

'Alesha,' she informed him matter-of-factly.

'Have you eaten?'

'I'm about to.' It would take only minutes to assemble a salad and enjoy her solitary meal. 'Why?'

'I'll collect you in ten minutes.'

Who does he think he is? *Don't go there.*

'If you're issuing an invitation,' she managed silkily, 'it's polite to request, not demand.'

'I'll make a note of it.'

Was there a smidgen of mild amusement apparent in his response?

'Ten minutes.' He cut the connection, and left her silently fuming and on the verge of calling back to insist she meet him at a nominated venue.

Except it would seem petty, and not the action of a woman in control. Or one determined to treat this meeting with prosaic common sense.

There was the need to change. Comfortable well-worn jeans, a casual top, her dark hair caught in a careless knot and anchored there with a large clip, bare feet, and no make-up didn't comprise fitting attire in which to dine out.

There was a part of her that felt inclined to slip her feet into trainers, collect her car keys, wallet, and leave.

Except her absence wouldn't achieve a thing.

So, get over it, she admonished silently as she changed into tailored trousers and a buttoned blouse. She added a dash of colour to her lips, fixed her hair, then selected a fashionable jacket and slid her feet into killer heels.

Her intercom buzzed as she collected a clutch purse, and she picked up, clarified Loukas Andreou's image on the security monitor, then uttered a brisk—'I'm on my way down.'

His height and breadth of shoulder seemed vaguely intimidating, his hard, strong-boned facial features arresting in the early evening light. Black tailored trousers, a white shirt unbuttoned at the neck, and a black butter-soft leather jacket lent a casual sophisticated look…one she knew to be deceiving, given the power he wielded in the business arena.

'Loukas.' Her greeting was polite, almost formal as dark eyes seared her own, and for a moment she experienced the strangest feeling that time stood still. Then it was gone.

'Shall we get this over and done with?'

Was that a faint edge of humour apparent, or simply a trick of the light? She couldn't be sure in the brief instant before he stood to one side and indicated the black Aston Martin parked in the forecourt.

She walked at his side to the car, aware of his close proximity as he opened the passenger door and saw her seated before crossing to slip in behind the wheel.

There was an unwanted sense of nervousness she strove hard to hide as he fired the engine and eased the powerful car onto the road.

A shared meal, during which she'd state her perspective, negotiate…and hopefully resolve the terms of Dimitri's will to their mutual satisfaction.

In a short space of time Loukas drew the Aston Martin to a halt at the entrance to the Ritz-Carlton hotel and organized valet parking.

Pleasant choice, Alesha approved, having dined in the restaurant on a few occasions.

Except once inside the foyer Loukas indicated the lift.

'My suite will afford us some privacy.'

Her nerve-ends coiled in painful protest at the thought of being alone with him. 'I'd prefer the restaurant.'

'And risk public scrutiny?' he elaborated

quietly. 'Possibly be overheard or photographed discussing a private matter?'

The fact that he was right didn't help much. Speculation would run rife soon enough when Loukas Andreou's continued presence in Sydney was noted. Especially when his extensive share-holding in Karsouli became known.

There was little she could do but acquiesce, albeit with some reluctance, duly observed, she noted as she bore Loukas' slightly hooded gaze as they rode the lift to his designated floor.

You can do this, a silent voice bade as she watched Loukas swipe a card and usher her into his suite. Loukas had her late father's trust. Otherwise Dimitri would never have structured his will the way he had.

Would he?

Dear God, how would she know…for sure?

With both parents gone, she had become very selective in whom she chose to confide in. Not even Lacey, a dear friend from childhood, knew everything about her first marriage. Some details were too personal…too hurtful to divulge.

'Relax,' Loukas drawled. 'I'm not about to hit on you.'

Alesha directed him a level look. 'I would deal with it if you did.' Hadn't she trained hard to effectively do so?

He shrugged out of his jacket, tossed it onto the large king-size bed, then he undid the cuffs on his shirt and turned them back twice, revealing muscular forearms sprinkled with dark hair.

'Can I take your jacket?'

'I'm fine, thanks.'

'Why don't you take a seat?' He indicated a comfortable chair. 'Would you like something to drink?'

'Can we pass on the social niceties and go straight to the matter at hand?'

He regarded her carefully for several long seconds, and she glimpsed a muscle tighten at the edge of his jaw.

'By all means,' he concurred with deliberate indolence. 'Then we'll eat.'

Alesha was so tempted to vent. Anger had built to a point where throwing a hissy fit would at least relieve some of her angst. Yet, conversely, it was probably exactly what he expected of her.

'The terms of my father's will are unconscionable.'

He didn't pretend to misunderstand. 'Apropos the marriage clause?'

'You *agree* with it?' Her eyes widened measurably. 'What manner of man are you?'

'One who prefers to embark on marriage with an honest foundation at its base.'

The look she gave him should have shrivelled him on the spot. Except it had no effect whatsoever.

'Oh…*please*. Let's not forget the primary focus.'

'Karsouli?'

Alesha allowed herself a faintly bitter smile. 'Dimitri's trump card.'

Loukas offered a thoughtful look. 'Perhaps.'

She stilled, suddenly alert. 'What are you saying?'

'Dimitri made a few errors in financial judgement in recent months.'

Her shock was real and barely masked. 'I don't believe you.'

'The global economic climate worked against him, so too did his failing health.'

Failing health? 'He was killed in a car accident.'

Loukas' gaze didn't waver. 'Your father risked heart failure unless he agreed to undergo heart transplant surgery. He refused, and bartered a deal with me to safeguard Karsouli.' He waited a beat. 'And you.'

No. The word echoed as a silent scream, and the blood chilled in her veins.

Oh, dear God.

'Karsouli needed a large injection of cash in order to remain solvent.'

'How much?' The demand almost choked her.

'Half a billion dollars.'

That much?

Selling off a twenty-five-per-cent share represented the injection of cash. The gift via Dimitri's will, conditional on marriage, would have been a sufficiently attractive enticement.

Karsouli would survive and flourish beneath Loukas Andreou's skilled leadership.

Of which she would become a joint partner and director. There was just one major snag… In order to achieve both, she had to agree to marry Loukas Andreou.

Two pluses versus one minus.

Alesha took a deep calming breath…not that it had any effect. 'I'll need to verify those facts.'

'Of course. I have certified copies of relevant documentation for you to peruse.'

Somehow she didn't expect any less of him. Even given the advantage of his father's success, Loukas appeared very much an achiever determined to forge his own destiny, both professionally and personally.

She accepted the paperwork, took time to read and absorb the data, aware of a sinking heart with every page.

The slim hope there might be a mistake disappeared as she was forced to face the inevitable.

With care she placed the papers onto the table,

then met his hooded gaze. 'Why did you sanction Dimitri's terms?'

One eyebrow lifted. 'The truth? His request coincided with a promise I had made to my own father to marry and provide an heir.'

'How noble,' Alesha accorded sweetly. 'To sacrifice yourself out of duty and family loyalty.' She sharpened a figurative barb. 'Were none of the many women who attach themselves to you suitable wife material?'

His features assumed musing cynicism. 'No.'

'What if I choose to contest the marriage clause?'

His eyes speared her own, dark with dangerous intent, and belying the quiet purpose in his voice.

'Should you refuse, the purchase will fall through. I'll sell the twenty-five-per-cent shares comprising Dimitri's bequest, and you will be placed in an invidious financial position.'

Forced to take on a partner and possibly face a takeover bid. Thereby losing everything her father had achieved. All she'd lived and breathed for as long as she could remember.

Anger, resentment, dammit—*grief*, welled up inside. So many emotions…consuming, invasive, and in that moment uncontrolled.

She stood and turned towards the door. 'Go to hell.'

CHAPTER TWO

'I SUGGEST you *think* before you walk out that door,' Loukas cautioned with dangerous quietness. 'Or the *hell* you'd consign me to will be your own.'

His meaning was icily clear, and had a sobering effect.

Pride and anger held no place in Dimitri's diabolical scheme.

Walk...and Alesha would lose the *one* thing she considered to be the most important entity in her life.

Could she trust Loukas? Dear heaven. If not him...*who*?

At least he had a vested interest in Karsouli; he possessed the skill and expertise to assume dual directorship; add considerable financial resources...

It was no contest.

Except she was damned if she'd give in easily.

For the space of a few seconds she closed her eyes, then opened them again, took a deep calming breath and turned slowly to face him.

There was an inherent strength apparent, an entity that went deep beneath the surface. An indomitable sense of power that made him both an invaluable ally and feared adversary.

But as a husband? *Lover?*

An instant recall of what she'd suffered at Seth's hands sent apprehension feathering her spine.

Don't go there.

One man's manic proclivities were not those of all men.

Unbidden, her teeth worried the inner fullness of her lower lip.

Yet how could she *know* for sure?

Seth had played the perfect part as loving fiancé, adoring new husband…until she had refused to concede to his demands.

A sudden bleakness clouded her eyes. A shadow of pain which appeared so fleetingly Loukas almost missed it, and his gaze narrowed.

'If the deal didn't include *marriage*, I'd be ecstatic.'

'Nevertheless, it does.'

'Unfortunately.'

On some level she *got* the loyalty thing. Matchmaking suitable partners from two eminently suitable families. A little devious manipulation added to the mix, and *voilà*…the convenient marriage scenario intended to safeguard the family fortunes and ensure the continuation of a dynasty.

'Yes or no, Alesha.' His expression was unreadable, his eyes dark and unwavering as they regarded her.

It had to be *yes*. There was no way she could countenance Karsouli slipping ignominiously between the cracks to disappear in the belly of iniquity.

'I have no choice but to agree, subject to certain conditions.'

There was a strength apparent in her demeanour, a determination he could only admire given she'd taken a king-hit about the true state of her father's corporation.

'Name them.' His voice held a silkiness she chose to ignore.

'I retain my position in Karsouli.'

Loukas inclined his head in agreement. 'Naturally.'

Now for the cruncher. 'A separate suite of rooms in whatever home we share.'

His gaze narrowed. 'Your reason being?'

She kept her eyes steady on his. 'A personal preference.'

'Based on?'

'A need for my own space.'

He regarded her in silence for several timeless

seconds. 'The same bedroom, separate beds.' He waited a beat. 'Until you feel comfortable sharing mine.'

As if that were going to happen any time soon. 'It isn't fair you get to dictate all the terms.'

'Be grateful I've conceded one of them.'

But not for long. Apprehension rose like a spectre, and for one wild moment she wondered at her sanity in aligning herself with a man such as him.

'So, on that basis, I should fawn at your feet and express undying gratitude?'

A faint quirk lifted the corner of his mouth. 'For saving Karsouli?'

'Of course.' Her response held a certain dryness that didn't fool him in the slightest.

Honesty, at a cost. With no attempt to hide it beneath any number of platitudes. Strength and a degree of fragility, he mused, made for an intriguing mix.

Loukas retrieved the in-room dining menu, opened it at the appropriate page and handed it to her. 'Choose what you'd like, and I'll order dinner.'

Food? The mere thought of ingesting anything was enough to send her stomach into immediate revolt.

'I'm not hungry.' What was more, she wanted

out of here. Away from this forceful man who held her fate in his hands.

She caught up her bag and slung the strap over one shoulder. 'I should leave.'

His eyes seared hers. 'We're not done.'

She took the few steps to move past him, only to come to a halt mere inches from where he stood. 'Yes, we are.'

'We'll share a meal, discuss wedding arrangements and relevant details, then I'll return you to your apartment.'

Alesha tilted her head a little. 'So…sit down, be quiet, and bow my head in polite servitude?'

She could almost swear she caught a faint gleam of humour on his handsome face, but then it was gone. 'I doubt the latter two form part of your repertoire.'

'How perceptive of you.' Sweet, she could do sweet, although it was impossible he missed the faint edge apparent in her voice.

Loukas offered her the menu. 'Choose, Alesha. Or I'll order for you.'

A starter would be all she could manage, and she selected one, then attempted to tune out as he picked up the phone.

A difficult feat, when the fine edge of awareness curled around her nerve-ends and heightened the tension she experienced in his presence.

A sophisticated strategist, he bore the persona of a man well versed in the ways of humankind, with the ability to see through any deliberate orchestration.

Had anyone tested his control…and escaped unscathed?

Stupid question. Why even go there? Loukas Andreou was an entity unto himself…indomitable, inviolate, and utterly ruthless.

But what of the essence of the man…as a friend, lover, husband? Would he be capable of gifting a degree of affection? *Caring?*

Or would she merely become a trophy wife… soothed by an enviable lifestyle and expensive gifts? Her life a mere facsimile?

The question had to be, was retaining Karsouli worth a marriage she didn't want to a man who placed financial assets above all else?

Get over yourself, she denounced in silent chastisement. You thought you had *love* first time round, only to discover to your cost that it was nothing more than a nebulous dream.

At least marriage to Loukas would be unclouded by sentiment. A business arrangement she entered into with her eyes wide open… nothing more, nothing less.

Their meal, when it arrived, was beautifully presented, although Alesha barely tasted a thing as she forked morsels of food with mechanical precision.

'I have the application for a special licence,' Loukas informed her as they shared coffee. 'It requires your signature. I foresee the marriage ceremony going ahead on Friday.'

'This Friday?'

His eyes seared her own. 'Is that a problem?'

You're joking, right?

'Why the hurry?' she managed, and quelled the sudden onset of nerves playing havoc with her stomach as he queried reasonably,

'Why delay?'

Sure, and she was ready for this?

Take a *reality* check. A week, a month—even a year down the track, and she'd still never be *ready* to embark on another marriage.

Yet ever present was the instinctive knowledge there would be no second chance with Loukas if she reneged.

'Give me the application and a pen.'

She attached her signature with a sense of fatalism, then she reached for her shoulder bag, slid the strap over one shoulder and purposely made for the door. 'I'll call a taxi.'

Loukas stood, filched his jacket from the back of the chair, then he hooked it over one shoulder and reached the door ahead of her.

Okay, he could accompany her to the lift, except when it had been summoned he accompanied her into the electronic cubicle.

Courtesy was a fine thing, she acknowledged as they reached the ground floor, and she turned towards him prior to moving across the foyer. 'Goodnight.'

Without a further word she crossed to the concierge desk and made a polite but firm request, which was negated by Loukas' presence.

'The lady is with me,' he informed the concierge, and followed it with a request for his car to be brought up from valet parking.

Alesha opened her mouth to deny it, only for Loukas to direct her a piercing look. 'Don't argue.'

'There's no need—'

'Yes, there is.'

It was ridiculous, and her eyes flashed dark fire before she lowered her lashes to hide her anger at his high-handedness.

'Did you have to behave like a dictatorial ass?' Alesha demanded the instant he eased the sleek Aston Martin out onto the street.

'That's a first.' His drawled comment held a tinge of humour she chose to ignore.

'So, bite me.'

'Aren't you in the least concerned I might bite back?'

She was unprepared for the faint sensation feathering over the surface of her skin as it stirred something deep inside she had no wish to disturb.

She didn't offer so much as a word during the short drive to her apartment, and she reached for the door-clasp the instant the car slid to a halt at the kerb.

Cool, polite words born from instilled good manners emerged from her lips. 'Thanks for the ride.'

She didn't wait for his acknowledgment, nor did she look back as she swiped her card at the main entry and hurried into the foyer.

It was a relief to enter her apartment, tend to the lock and security system.

Home. A place uniquely *hers*, where she felt safe, secure.

But not for long, a tiny voice taunted. All too soon her life…*everything* would change. She slipped off her stilettos, then discarded her jacket. It wasn't late, and she was too tense to consider retiring to bed.

Television, watching a DVD, or work were three options, and she retreated to her bedroom, discarded her clothes and donned cotton sleep trousers and a singlet top before cleansing off her make-up. Then she slotted in a DVD and settled into a comfortable chair with the remote.

It was almost midnight when the credits rolled,

and she switched everything off, then made her way to bed…surprisingly to sleep until the alarm roused her early next morning.

Maintaining a routine gave focus to the day, and Alesha donned sweats, slid her feet into trainers, tied back her hair, exited the apartment building and broke into a steady jog en route to a local gym.

An hour's workout helped diminish her stress levels, and she returned home with renewed vigour to shower, breakfast, then dress for work.

The executive power suit, minimum jewellery, hair smoothed into an upswept style, a light touch with make-up, killer heels…and she was good to go.

Laptop, briefcase, shoulder bag…check.

Minutes later she slid behind the wheel of her silver BMW, engaged the engine, then made her way to the main arterial road leading into the city.

Traffic at this hour was heavy, and making it through electronically controlled intersections without at least two enforced stops was rare.

Consequently it was almost eight when Alesha took the lift from the basement parking area to a high floor in the tall modern building housing the Karsouli Corporation.

A luxurious office suite with prime views over

the inner harbour, expensive carpeting, sparkling glass, executive furniture and expensive works of art adorning the walls.

Dimitri had enjoyed displaying the acquisitions earned by his success. Ongoing consultations with a prominent interior decorator ensured *ostentatious* didn't figure in the scheme of things.

Alesha didn't want anything to change. In fact, she'd insist on it. Karsouli would remain Karsouli in honour of her father's memory, his years of hard work.

'Good morning.' Her smile held genuine warmth as she passed through Reception and trod the wide passageway leading to her office.

A greeting she repeated as her PA rose from behind a desk with the day's scheduling in hand.

'Mr Andreou requests your presence a.s.a.p. An executive meeting will be chaired by Mr Andreou at ten in the conference room. Department heads are currently being advised. I've noted everything in your diary, and printed a copy for your perusal.'

Alesha took the offered schedule, skimmed it, and her eyes widened fractionally.

Loukas was wasting no time in setting several contingency plans in motion.

'Thanks, Anne. You can alert Mr Andreou I'll be with him in ten minutes.'

'I understand there is some urgency to his request.'

Sufficient for Anne to issue the caution? All hail the new chief? Except the partnership with Loukas was equal. And *damned* if she'd drop everything and rush to his bidding!

'Ten minutes, Anne.'

She took every one of them before entering the large office Dimitri had occupied for as long as she could remember…and tamped down the faint resentment she experienced at seeing Loukas seated behind her father's desk.

'You wanted to see me?' The polite smile she summoned didn't reach her eyes as Loukas rose to his feet and moved forward to close the door behind her.

An action that sent the nerves in her stomach into a tangled knot.

He indicated a leather chair. 'Take a seat.' Whereupon he crossed to the desk to lean one hip against its edge.

She continued to stand. 'I hope this won't take long.'

'You'd have preferred a memo relaying I'm due in Melbourne late this afternoon to head an emergency meeting before flying on to Adelaide, then the Gold Coast?'

'You require my input?'

'Personally or professionally?'

A trick question? 'Professionally, of course.'

Of course. His eyes narrowed a little as he took in the red power suit, the killer heels, the upswept hair, and his fingers itched to loosen the pins holding the elegantly contrived knot in place.

Her choice of apparel made a statement, one she'd deliberately sought to portray, he noted silently. And wondered why she'd thought it necessary.

Because she felt threatened by him? Perhaps she had cause, professionally.

'The current state of Karsouli requires swift action, and formal meetings with each of the men who head the corporation's three out-of-state offices are imperative. Personally, not via conference call.'

Alesha didn't give him the satisfaction of verbally agreeing with him. 'When will you be back?'

'Late Thursday evening.'

'I trust you'll keep me posted. Is that all?'

One eyebrow quirked a little. 'There's the matter of our wedding details.'

Her stomach executed a painful somersault, and it took considerable effort to remain calm. 'Email me the time and venue.'

'Wolseley Road, Point Piper.' He offered the number. 'Friday, four o'clock in the afternoon.'

A slight frown creased her forehead. 'That's a private residence.' Situated amongst Sydney's most expensive real estate.

'My home, which is currently in the final stages of redecoration.'

Sufficient money could achieve almost anything…and obviously had. It explained his preference for temporary hotel accommodation.

'There's also the legalities attached to the union,' Loukas relayed smoothly. 'We have an appointment at three-thirty this afternoon to tend to the necessary paperwork.'

Ensuring everything was neatly tied together before he flew out to Melbourne, she perceived, and attempted to quell the feeling she'd boarded a runaway train from which escape would involve irreparable damage to life and limb.

'Fine.'

'There's nothing you want to add?'

A whole heap in verbal castigation…none of which would do any good! Instead, she managed a stunningly sweet smile. 'Not at this moment.'

She turned and made for the door, only to discover he was there before her, and she attempted to ignore his close proximity, the musky tang of his cologne, the sheer sensuality he managed to exude without any seeming effort at all.

Assuring herself she was immune didn't quite cut it. Nor did likening him to *all* men.

Loukas Andreou stood alone, a male entity that defied categorization.

So where did that leave *her*?

Right now...out of here!

'Ten in the conference room,' Loukas reminded her silkily as she exited the room.

A meeting he chaired with the type of ruthless strategy that left no room for doubt his proposed restructuring of Karsouli would be immediate and far-reaching.

Details were provided in individual folders placed in front of the attending executives, who were each given forty-eight hours in which to submit approval, reservations...or otherwise.

It took considerable effort on Alesha's part to contain her resentment and present a neutral front when she wanted to silently rage at his high-handedness.

She managed it, *just*, until Loukas called the meeting to a close, and she bore the carefully polite glances as the executive staff filed past her as they exited the room.

Questions would follow by the long-serving personnel, concern expressed by those whose tenure was more recent...and she'd do her best with damage control.

But *now* she had a bone to pick with the self-appointed man in control.

With care she closed the door and crossed to where Loukas stood assembling paperwork into his briefcase.

'How dare you initiate changes without consulting me?'

She resembled a pocket virago, Loukas noted. Dark eyes flashed with anger as she sent him a venomous glare. 'My father—'

'Allowed his emotions to rule, and didn't keep you apprised of the reality.'

'You can't just terminate—'

'Dimitri kept performance details on file of every employee.' He handed her a memory stick. 'Study them in my absence, together with my recommendations, and we'll confer on my return.'

'And if I don't agree?'

'We'll discuss it.'

'*We* will?' The fine edge of sarcasm was evident. 'Should I express gratitude at being slotted into your busy schedule?'

His cellphone beeped and he checked the screen. 'I need to take this call. Three-thirty, Alesha. My office.'

The temptation to throw something at him was uppermost, and she deliberately held his dark gaze, glimpsed his recognition of her intent, together with his silent threat of retribution.

For a timeless few seconds the air between them pulsed with electricity, a perilous force so overwhelming she almost forgot to breathe.

Then he activated the call, effectively dismissing her.

Panache, control, she possessed both, and she turned away from him and exited the room, closing the door with an imperceptible click behind her, when she would have delighted in slamming it. Except the door was carefully weighted to avoid anything other than a smooth, almost silent action.

She wanted badly to vent, and she would the moment she had him alone, she promised as she crossed to her office.

Three-thirty couldn't appear soon enough!

CHAPTER THREE

ALESHA spent what remained of the morning attending to the immediate business at hand, and chose to have her PA send out for a chicken and salad sandwich with mayo on rye and a double-strength latte.

Something that became a working lunch eaten at her desk as she accessed computer data, inserted reference notations, took phone calls and instructed Anne to clear an hour between three-thirty and four-thirty.

The adherence to punctuality was something Alesha considered important…personally, and professionally. And *this* was business, she qualified as she allowed time to freshen up before presenting herself at Dimitri's…dammit, *Loukas'* office on time.

He stood close to the plate-glass window with its cityscape view of the inner harbour, cellphone at his ear in quiet conversation as he gestured she take a seat.

Contrarily she opted to remain standing, and she caught his faint gleam of amusement as he continued conversing in French…with a woman, from the light tone of his voice.

A lover? Past or present? Certainly a *close* friend.

She told herself she didn't care…and, in truth, she didn't. So how did she explain the sudden warmth flooding her veins, the slow invidious curling sensation deep within?

Because she envied the woman his affection-ate attention?

Oh, *please*. Get real. She no more wanted another man in her life than she wanted to fly over the moon.

Especially not *this* man. Impressive, too powerful, *too much*.

A slight shiver feathered the length of her spine. *Way* too much on a personal level.

Why not call it as it was? The forceful Greek exuded a magnetic sexuality that verged close to the primitive.

The sensual promise was *there*, almost a tangible entity, and for one wild moment she wondered what it would be like to be ravished beneath his hands, his mouth…dear God, his possession.

Soul-destroying. Utterly. Completely.

Enough already, she upbraided silently. Focus on the here and now.

Dimitri's office had undergone a few changes.

State-of-the-art electronic technology replaced the standard desktop her father had preferred, several files were stacked at the end of the desk, an MP3 player. Tidy, but very much the workspace of a busy man.

'Shall we leave?'

Alesha cast Loukas a deceptively cool glance as he pocketed his cellphone, collected a briefcase, laptop, and indicated she precede him from the room.

'I'll meet you at the lawyer's office,' she indicated as the lift transported them down to the underground parking area.

'We'll go together in my car.'

'It might be easier if I follow you.'

The lift doors slid open and Loukas shot her an analytical look as they entered the concrete cavern. 'Are you determined to debate me on every issue?'

The air sizzled with a tension she refused to define. She should cease and desist, but there was a dangerous imp sitting on her shoulder bent on mischief and mayhem.

'My apologies.' She offered him a sweet smile. 'I tend to forget most women merely *exist* to do your bidding.'

'But not you.' His drawled response held a tinge of humour.

'No,' she managed with a degree of dry

mockery. 'However, in this instance I'll concede and get a taxi back to the office when we're done.'

They reached the Aston Martin and he unsecured the locking mechanism to the doors, the trunk, deposited his briefcase and laptop, then closed the trunk. 'I'll drop you off before I continue on to the airport.'

'It's out of your way.'

'Get in the car, Alesha.' His voice held a silky quality that boded ill for further argument.

She slid into the passenger seat and waited until he moved in behind the wheel before posing with deliberate sweetness, 'Are you always so appallingly arrogant?'

He ignited the engine. 'Whenever the occasion demands.'

Inner-city traffic and numerous electronically-controlled intersections ensured it took fifteen minutes to cross town, a further five to find a parking bay beneath the lawyer's office building.

Alesha was conscious of Loukas' studied look as he jabbed the call-button summoning the lift, and she tilted her head a little as she held his gaze.

'What?' she challenged. 'My mascara is smudged? Too much bronzing powder or not enough?'

'Faultless.' His silky drawl held a tinge of amusement as the lift drew to a smooth halt.

'While you resemble the quintessential male,' she responded an instant before she preceded him into the spacious reception area.

Within a very short space of time she'd sign documentation detailing precise legalese pertaining to the terms outlined in Dimitri's will. A pre-nup covering every known contingency.

Copies of which she'd already perused.

So why *now* were the nerves in her stomach tying themselves in knots?

Because each step she took brought her closer to a marriage she didn't want. To a man she had no choice but to trust on every level.

Sure, she could opt out. Except losing Karsouli was too heavy a penalty to pay.

Consequently she listened to the lawyer's clarification, the reassurance he felt beholden to relay.

When he was done, she took up a proffered pen, signed where indicated, then solemnly watched as Loukas attached his signature.

'I consider it an honour to act as a witness to your marriage on Friday. Dimitri would be very pleased with this outcome.'

Alesha managed a faint smile at the lawyer's words.

What about *her*? Didn't she count? Or was she merely a pawn in a diabolical game?

Don't go there. It's done.

Almost.

Next step…marriage.

She preceded Loukas into the lift and pressed the 'ground' button on the instrument panel.

He stood too close as he chose 'basement', and when they reached street level he merely bypassed her command and sent the lift down.

Her mouth tightened and she cast him a fulminating glare…which had no effect whatsoever.

'Give it up,' Loukas advised as the lift doors slid open and he indicated the black Aston Martin.

He waited until they were both seated before engaging the engine. 'Can I leave the choice of second witness with you?'

There was only one person she'd consider asking. Lacey Pattison, lifelong friend and trusted confidante who had, ironically, acted as chief bridesmaid at her first wedding. 'Yes.'

Was there such a thing as the sound of silence? If so, it seemed to hang heavy in the car's interior as he negotiated city traffic before easing the car into the kerb adjacent the office tower housing Karsouli.

'You have my cellphone number if you have any concerns.'

She met his dark gaze with equanimity. 'Is this where I wish you a safe flight?'

The edge of his mouth quirked a little. 'I'll be in touch Thursday evening.'

'I might be otherwise engaged with a male stripper at a very private "hen" party.' *As if.*

'In which case, have fun.'

That was it? No macho follow-up?

'Not quite.'

He read minds?

The next instant he leant forward and took her mouth with his own in a slow evocative kiss that drained the breath from her body…and then some.

There was no demand, just a sense of intent…*his.*

Then he straightened, and his eyes narrowed at her faintly dazed expression, the sudden paleness of her cheeks.

In one fluid movement she released her seat belt, caught up her bag and slid out from the passenger seat before crossing to the building's foyer without so much as a backward glance.

It was only as she rode the lift that she permitted herself to reflect.

The feel of his mouth on her own lingered, and she pressed light fingers to her lips.

What was that?

No matter how she viewed it, there had been nothing to prepare her for the unexpected sensuality evident…or her reaction.

The unbidden need to deepen the kiss was

merely a transitory figment of her imagination, she dismissed as she entered Reception and moved into her office.

The phone call to Lacey resulted in a barrage of rapid-fire questions, to which only truthful answers would suffice.

'Okay,' Lacey said with deliberate calm. 'We've covered the *who, why, when* and *where*. I've done the *ohmigod* thing. Now it's down to basics. What are you going to wear?'

'I'm sure there's something suitable in my wardrobe.'

'We'll go shopping tomorrow afternoon.'

'Lacey—no.'

'*Yes.* Double Bay.' She named a place. 'I'll be there at three.'

'I don't finish until five.'

'You're the boss. Leave early.'

'You're impossible.'

'Yes, I know. That's why I'm your friend. *Three*, Alesha. Don't be late. We have a lot of ground to cover in a short time.'

She opened her mouth to protest, except the faint click indicated Lacey had already hung up.

The next morning Alesha went into the office early, declined a lunch break and collected Lacey mid-afternoon to shop for *the* dress.

'Coffee first, double shot of caffeine, double sugar,' Alesha determined as Lacey indicated one of a few streets in exclusive Double Bay where boutiques offered designer wear with exorbitant price tags.

'Darling, *no*.' Lacey gave her a *don't mess with me* look Alesha recognized from old. 'Dress first, coffee later.'

'I need sustenance.'

'Delaying tactics,' Lacey dismissed. 'We're shopping for your *wedding dress*. Something that cannot be rushed. We need to *look*.'

'*One* boutique,' Alesha stated firmly. 'I choose, try it on, present plastic, we leave.'

Lacey's smile was pure imp dressed in steel. 'You think?'

Alesha achieved an expressive eye-roll. 'I *knew* inviting you was asking for trouble.'

'Precisely why you displayed *some* sense,' came the airy response. '*Chill*,' her friend commanded as they paused outside a small boutique with one model displayed in the window. 'Let's go inspect the merchandise, shall we?'

She uttered an expressive sigh. 'I don't think—'

'You don't *need* to think while I'm here to advise and guide.'

'That's what concerns me.'

The vendeuse greeted them with refined politeness, whereupon Lacey launched into her verbal spiel.

'White, of course.'

'Ivory,' Alesha corrected.

'Full-length,' Lacey insisted.

'Mid-calf.'

'Stunning.'

She did the eye-roll thing. 'Simple.'

'Perhaps it would help if you tell me something about the venue, the reception, the number of guests,' the vendeuse suggested.

'A civil ceremony held in a private home with two witnesses.'

'Ah. I see.' There was a faint click of the fingers as she accurately appraised Alesha's slim curves. 'I think I can offer you something suitable.'

The design was fine, the colour was not.

'It's a very pale blush.'

'Thank you, but no.'

The second boutique had the perfect gown, Chanel...except it only came in black. Alesha considered, only to be firmly outvoted by Lacey. 'You are *not* getting married in *black*.'

'Hey, whose wedding is this, anyway?'

'Yours, and just because it's not traditional, doesn't mean we won't do it *right*. Agreed?'

Lacey had a point. 'Coffee,' Alesha insisted.

'Soon, promise. Let's go.'

'Heaven forbid…*where*? I thought we had a one-stop deal.'

Lacey took hold of her arm and led the way to the car.

'Get in and drive.'

'It had better be good.'

Doing it right was achieved in a beautiful little boutique that sold vintage designer gear. Gorgeous gowns in cream, ivory…and Alesha sighed as she caught sight of sheer perfection. A slim-fitting gown in layered ivory and pale champagne silk, accented by a fine pin-tucking edged with narrow lace.

'Delicate strappy sandals with killer heels,' Lacey advised. 'Minimum jewellery, just diamond ear-studs. Maybe a bracelet.'

Alesha removed the gown, handed it to the sales person, endeavoured not to blink at the price, presented plastic and minutes later walked from the shop with a signature-emblazoned glossy carry-bag.

'Strappy sandals,' Lacey insisted. 'Then we get to have coffee. OK?'

'Thanks.' She gave her friend an impulsive heart-felt hug. 'I couldn't have done this without you.'

A light bubbling laugh emerged as Lacey initiated a high-five gesture. 'Who else, when we've been friends since for ever?'

'Sisters in every way but by blood.' *There* for each other, the first one to call.

It was later as they sat sharing coffee that Lacey adopted a serious expression. 'You so deserve to be happy.'

Alesha smiled. 'Wisdom over double-shot lattes?'

'Loukas is a good guy.'

She slanted an eyebrow. 'And you know this… because?'

'I've met him, remember? He made a lasting impression.'

Alesha took time to sip her coffee. 'That's supposed to be reassurance?'

'He's hot. Those eyes. That mouth.' Lacey gave a lascivious sigh. 'Yum…and then some.'

'*Yum?*' she queried with quizzical amusement.

'Uh-huh.'

A wicked smile widened her lips. 'I think you need food. Plus, I owe you, big time. Let's do dinner…my treat.'

Lacey laughed with delight. '*Where?*'

'Your choice.'

'Reckless. Definitely reckless.' Lacey allowed a few seconds' deliberation. 'Italian. There's this little restaurant that serves divine pasta to die for. It's the other side of town.'

Alesha rose to her feet and paid the tab. 'Let's go.'

It became a wonderfully relaxing few hours as they enjoyed fine food, a glass of wine, reminisced and laughed.

True friendship was something to be treasured, and Alesha entered her apartment at evening's end with a lighter heart.

The familiar nightmare came out of nowhere in the early pre-dawn hours, vivid, almost *live* in its intensity, and she woke breathing hard, her body soaked with sweat.

She reached for the bedside lamp and the room glowed with light.

Dear God.

She lifted a hand to her face, almost expecting in that instant to feel the heat, the swelling, the *pain*. Except her cheeks were cool, and for several long moments she worked at slowing her breathing, her rapidly beating pulse.

A silent voice prompted… *You're fine.*

In the here and *now*…and alone.

With one smooth movement she cast aside the covers and padded out to the kitchen, brewed tea, then she subsided into a comfortable chair and channel-surfed until she found a comedy and didn't move until the dawn gradually lightened the sky from indigo to pearl grey.

Then she hit the shower and dressed. Breakfast was yoghurt and fruit with a reviving shot of caffeine, before she fixed her make-up, gathered her laptop, bag, keys, and drove into the city.

Focus, concentrate on the day, Alesha urged as she rode the lift to the high floor housing Karsouli.

As days went, this one soon became a doozy, with her PA calling in sick, the replacement hesitant to take any initiative, minor delays resulting therefrom, and a laptop that decided to crash at a crucial moment. Fortunately the auto-save function ensured only a small amount of data was lost, but it took time to get the system up and running again…time that became increasingly scarce as the day progressed.

Consequently she skipped lunch, alternated coffee with bottled water, and made do with a banana mid-afternoon.

Running on empty was not advisable, and coupled with loss of sleep it tipped her into headache territory with increasing intensity.

At five she was tempted to give up, except another hour—two, tops—and she'd put the day's work to bed. Given international time-zones, the data would be accessible, and any delay minimal.

She was almost done when her cellphone buzzed, and she automatically picked up…something she rarely did without first checking caller ID.

'Alesha.'

There was no mistaking that deep, faintly accented voice. 'Hi.' As a greeting, it was sadly lacking.

'I'm on my way up.'

So he was back…and *here*. He'd said he'd call, but she hadn't counted on seeing him. Nor did she expect the slow curling sensation to begin deep within.

She wasn't alone in the building… There would be others staying back catching up on work, the cleaning staff.

Minutes later he was there, his tall frame filling the aperture, and unbidden her pulse kicked into a faster beat as he moved into her office.

'Working late?'

His voice was deceptively mild, his eyes faintly hooded as he took in her pale features, the dark circles beneath her eyes. She looked beat, almost fragile, and at a guess she was harbouring a headache.

Alesha deliberately focused her attention on the computer screen. 'And you're here…why?'

'I need to collect a file which hasn't been uploaded into the computer system.'

A mark against Dimitri's recently reassigned PA?

Her father had expected efficiency…but not to the level demanded beneath Loukas' direction.

'Tough day?'

Like you wouldn't believe. 'I'm almost done.'

'Good. You can share Chinese with me.'

She lifted her head and saw the paper sack he placed on her desk. 'You brought food?' Her stomach did a slow roll in anticipatory pleasure.

'I missed lunch.' And opted out of an in-flight meal that failed to provide sufficient sustenance to fuel a minimum four hours' work. Following an intense few days of meetings, staff reorganization, and ironing out several kinks in the Karsouli infrastructure.

He thrived on brokering high-powered deals, but Karsouli was personal. Aware of the need for a different approach from the *slash and burn* techniques for which he'd gained a formidable reputation.

The necessity to input a few hours' work didn't faze him. What he hadn't expected to see when he entered the office building's underground parking area was Alesha's silver BMW stationary in its parking bay.

Loukas heard her faint sigh as she hit *save* and closed down. With deft movements he snapped open the various containers and handed her a set of chopsticks.

'Eat.'

She did, with evident enjoyment. 'Thanks. This is so much better than a boiled egg and salad.'

'No girls' night out?'

'The male stripper called in sick.' Her response was slick, and she was almost sure she caught a faint gleam of humour apparent in his dark eyes.

'No replacement available?'

'Unfortunately.'

His presence unsettled her. There was something about him…a dangerous sexual chemistry combined with a primitive earthy quality that promised much.

It filled her with a curious tension, combining reluctant anticipation with a sense of trepidation.

Which seemed crazy. She didn't even *like* him.

Or was that due to an emotional shutdown… hers? A case of 'if you don't think about it, it won't happen'.

Some chance.

She should leave.

With that thought in mind, she gathered her jacket, her laptop and briefcase. 'You have work to do.'

He stood up. 'I'll see you down to the car.'

'That's not necessary.'

He merely slanted an eyebrow and indicated she precede him. 'I consider it is.'

She was tempted to argue. Instead she summoned a sweet smile. 'How…' she paused, then added with delicate intent '…kind.'

Her eyes widened as he trailed light fingers down her cheek in an unexpected gesture that stole the breath from her throat.

'Get some sleep.' Then he dropped his hand, and she stood still for a few heart-stopping seconds before brushing past him.

Thankfully the lift doors opened the instant she pressed the call-button, and she moved in ahead of him, then stood in silence as the cubicle transported them swiftly down to basement level.

It took only minutes to reach her car, and she released the locking mechanism, slid behind the wheel, engaged the ignition and drove towards the ramp leading to street level without a backwards glance.

Traffic in the inner city had eased from its peak-hour exodus, and she reached her apartment with a sense of relief.

A hot shower, attired in sleepwear, a cup of tea plus a couple of painkillers in hand, she curled up in a comfortable chair to watch TV for an hour or two before she retired for the night.

On the edge of sleep came the intrusive knowledge that tomorrow she would marry Loukas.

Share his home, his bed, eventually.

How long would he allow her solitary occupation in a bed next to his own? A few nights... a week?

Did it matter?

She told herself she didn't care. Sex was just… sex. In the dark of night she could simply close her eyes and wait for the act to be over.

How difficult could it be?

CHAPTER FOUR

Two wedding days three years apart, Alesha mused as she put the finishing touches to her make-up. Each so completely different they were at opposite ends of the spectrum!

Having *done* the full bridal thing with designer dress, four bridesmaids, flower girl, page boy, the church, several hundred guests, the tiered wedding cake and exclusive reception with her marriage to Seth, the prospect of a civil ceremony by a celebrant held in the grounds of the groom's Point Piper home with Dimitri's lawyer and Lacey as witnesses seemed a breeze by comparison.

So why was she a mass of nerves?

'You look gorgeous.' Lacey's compliment was genuine, and should have acted as reassurance. Instead the nerves inside Alesha's stomach twisted into a tighter ball.

'Thanks.'

Lacey looked at the overnight bag resting at the end of the bed. 'Is that all you're taking with you?'

'It's enough for the weekend.'

'Darling,' Lacey chided. 'You're *moving* in with Loukas. Permanently. You need to *pack*.'

'I'll shift some of my stuff tomorrow.'

'Hello?' The admonishment held a degree of musing scepticism.

Arguing with Lacey was a losing battle as her friend flung open wardrobe doors, drawers, and quickly transferred a varied assortment of apparel into a suitcase.

'Okay, we're out of here.'

Second thoughts? She had a few! Primarily, relating to her sanity!

Yet as tempting as it would be to bail out, there was the overriding knowledge that she'd *agreed* to this marriage. What was more, she'd signed legal documentation confirming it.

So *suck it up*, Alesha chastised as she negotiated traffic and headed towards suburban Point Piper, with Lacey following close behind.

Loukas' home was positioned behind a high wall and entered between stylish gates that opened onto a curved driveway leading to a double-storeyed mansion whose imposing entry was guarded by two massive ornamental-studded wooden doors.

She brought the BMW to a smooth halt behind a late-model four-wheel drive, and Lacey parked directly behind her.

No sooner had she cut the engine than both entry doors opened to reveal Loukas in the wide aperture.

His tall, broad-shouldered frame attired in an immaculate dark suit appeared slightly intimidating as he moved towards her.

There was little she could do to control the sudden fluttering inside her stomach as he held open the door for her to emerge.

'Alesha.' His close proximity, his dark watchful gaze merely accelerated her nervous tension, for soon, within the space of an hour or less, she'd enter into a legal union with this man…and her life would change.

Concern as to just *how* it would change affected her more than she imagined possible.

Would Loukas suddenly assume another identity within hours of the wedding…as Seth had?

The mere thought was enough to send an element of fear shivering the length of her spine, and the smile she summoned appeared over-bright and failed to reach her eyes.

Did he notice? She hoped not.

The faint sound of an engine caught her attention, and she turned slightly as a vehicle slid to a halt behind Lacey's car.

'The gang's all here.' She kept her voice light as Lacey joined them, followed closely by Dimitri's lawyer.

Loukas ushered them into a spacious foyer whose floor featured beautiful marble tiling in a large circular star-burst design, above whose centre an exquisite crystal chandelier provided prisms of light.

Antique tables, exquisitely crafted chairs, wall sconces, paintings, graced an area whose focal point was a sweeping double marble staircase featuring ornate wrought-iron balustrades leading to an upper floor balcony that divided into two separate galleried wings showcased by matching ornate wrought-iron balustrades.

'Come through to the lounge,' Loukas directed with ease. 'Everything is set up there.'

Alesha moved on autopilot, so acutely conscious of his presence at her side that she barely noticed the beautiful sofas and chairs, the amazingly high ceilings.

Instead she focused on the small table with its exquisite lace-edged linen cloth, the votive candle, a delicate spray of cream orchids, and a leather-bound Bible.

Introductions complete, the celebrant conferred with the lawyer, exchanged small talk, then she opted to begin the ceremony.

You can do this.

As an affirmation, it didn't begin to scratch the surface!

Almost as if he knew, Loukas captured her hand and held it loosely within his own.

To prevent her sudden need to escape? It was a moot point!

Alesha heard the solemn beautifully spoken words, and on some level she took them in, and managed to recite the vows that united her with Loukas in matrimony…aware his vows held a calm solemnity that was lacking in her own.

He slid a wide diamond-studded ring onto her finger, surprised her by lifting her hand and brushing the ring with his lips, before offering a ring for her to slip onto his finger.

He was prepared to wear a wedding ring?

Her fingers shook a little as she slid it on, and his hand covered hers as he used a little pressure to slide it home.

'It gives me great pleasure to pronounce you husband and wife.' The celebrant bestowed the gathered foursome a pleasant smile. 'And introduce Alesha and Loukas Andreou.' Loukas lifted both hands and cradled Alesha's head, then he covered her mouth with his own in a fleeting sensual caress.

Oh, my. There had to be some explanation for

the slow curl of sensation unfurling deep within her. Almost as if her body was at variance with the dictates of her mind.

How could she even begin to think what it would be like to have him invite a more intimate touch, to feel his hands on her body, his lips tasting an evocative trail, teasing, encouraging her response.

The question had to be *could* he succeed? When she'd left Seth she'd locked the door to her emotional heart and thrown away the key. And vowed never to allow another man to get close.

Alesha became conscious of Lacey's laughter as she was enveloped in a hug; the voiced congratulations from the lawyer, the celebrant; Loukas' hand resting against the back of her waist before he released her to open the champagne cooling in an ice bucket.

Smile, a silent voice prompted. You're supposed to be happy. The future of Karsouli is secure, and your future is safe…if *safe* could be attributed to the man whose ring she now wore.

So play the game expected of you. *Pretend.* Haven't the past few years provided plenty of practice?

Consequently she accepted a flute of champagne, smiled at the toast Lacey proposed to happiness and a blessed future, and managed to nibble a proffered canapé from a silver platter presented by Loukas' housekeeper, Eloise.

The celebrant took her leave, and conversation flowed with ease for a while until the lawyer indicated a pressing engagement and Lacey followed suit as she pressed a light kiss to Alesha's cheek before turning to Loukas.

'Take good care of her.'

'I intend to do so.'

Together they moved through the foyer to the main entrance where Loukas opened the door.

'Drive carefully.'

'Always.'

There was the sound of heels tapping along the driveway, the beep of a security remote, followed by the solid clunk of a car door closing and the purr of an engine as Lacey drove away.

Alesha watched as the car eased down the driveway, saw the accented red of brake lights as Lacey slowed at the gates, then the car disappeared from sight.

She was extremely conscious of the man who stood at her side, his easy movements as he closed both doors and activated the security system.

The house…*mansion*, she corrected, seemed incredibly large, not to mention an unknown entity, for, although she assumed the bedroom

suites were situated upstairs, she had no idea precisely which wing contained the master suite.

Loukas indicated the curved staircase. 'Eloise
will have transferred your bag upstairs.'

'Is this the part where you give me a guided tour?'

'You'd prefer to explore on your own?'

She crossed to the staircase and began ascending the wide marble stairs, aware he joined her.
'I might get lost.'

'It's quite simple. Personal suites and home
office situated to the left, guest suites to the right.
Ground floor, formal and informal lounge and
dining rooms, media, home theatre, kitchen, util-
ities. Lower floor, gym, entertainment room,
indoor pool. Outdoor pool. Self-contained flat
for staff over detached garages.'

They reached the gallery and turned to the left.
'It's a large home for one man.' An observation
that incurred his steady appraisal.

'A man who has very recently acquired a wife,'
he reminded silkily.

Loukas opened a set of double-panelled doors
to reveal a spacious master bedroom, containing
two king-size beds.

So he'd kept his word.

She told herself she should be relieved…and she
was. Except sharing the same room implied a
certain intimacy with which she felt distinctly un-

comfortable. There were two separate en suites, two dressing rooms and a recessed alcove furnished with two comfortable chairs and standard lamps.

It was, she had to admit, incredible. Luxurious, with spectacular views over the harbour to the cityscape. Magic at nightfall when the city was lit up and varied coloured neon flashed with advertisements atop many of the inner-city buildings.

He shrugged out of suit jacket, dispensed with his tie and loosened the top button of his shirt.

For a moment she caught her breath at his intention, and he glimpsed the fleeting apprehension evident before it was quickly masked.

'You might want to change into something less formal.'

She reminded him of a skittish foal in an unfamiliar environment...one who had experienced fear, possibly damage, with every reason to mistrust.

'Eloise has unpacked your bag.' Loukas indicated the dressing room she would use. 'Tomorrow we'll shift the remainder of your belongings.'

'I can manage on my own.'

'You won't need to.'

So give up the independent streak, accept two pairs of hands are better than one, and some masculine strength for the bag-carrying is a *good* thing.

Slipping into something more comfortable depended on what items of clothing Lacey packed, and she crossed into her allocated dressing room to check the meagre assortment.

Jeans didn't cut it, but tailored trousers with a cotton top would do.

Minutes later she emerged to find Loukas standing close to the wide expanse of glass taking in the panoramic scene.

The white shirt accentuated the impressive breadth of his shoulders, and his shirt cuffs had been folded back to rest midway up his forearms, lending a casual air.

Deceptive, she knew, for he could move with the silent stealth of a primitive cat and reduce an adversary to speechlessness with a few sententious words.

She watched as he turned towards her, and the breath caught in her throat.

He was someone she'd known for a number of years, as the son of Dimitri's closest friend, a man whose company she'd shared with her parents' friends and business associates on a few occasions at various social events. Instinctively aware, even then, that when he played, he played to win…in business, and with women.

Through circumstance he'd won Karsouli... together with her as part of the package.

'Shall we go eat?'

Food wasn't foremost on her mind, although she sipped excellent vintage wine, sampled succulent morsels from no less than three courses, while engaging in meaningless conversation.

The economic state of the nation and the world's foremost leaders made for interesting debate and carried the hour with relative ease. Something for which she was immensely grateful.

'Do you still have regular contact with Lacey?'

Alesha wondered if Loukas' query related to genuine interest, or merely a shift to the more personal.

'Regularly,' she answered lightly. 'We share dinner each week, occasionally take in a movie. Go shopping together.'

'I seem to recall you were a keen advocate of tennis. Do you still play?'

'Not as often as I used to.' She took an appreciative sip of fine wine. 'Do you still travel extensively?'

'My father prefers to remain in Greece these days.' He affected a slight shrug. 'Andreou has offices in London, Milan and New York, and I alternate between each of them while overseeing the main office in Athens.'

'And now you've added Sydney to the equation.'

One eyebrow lifted in sardonic query. 'That still bothers you?'

'I have no alternative but to accept it.'

'It's a little late to change your mind.'

'How are your parents? Your sister Lexi?'

'They're well. My mother is on various committees, which consume some of her time. Lexi designs handcrafted jewellery and has a studio in the Pláka.'

'And your Aunt Daria?' It was a polite query and resulted in a musing smile.

'She remains a force to be reckoned with.'

Plain-spoken to the point of bluntness, Alesha remembered as she recalled a visit to Athens with her parents several years ago when they'd spent time with Angelina and Constantine Andreou.

'That appears to take care of family and friends,' Alesha managed lightly. 'Should we move on to the more personal? The master breeding plan, perhaps? I trust you're aware the male sperm determine the sex of the child?' She spared him a pseudo-intelligent look. 'I refuse to bear any blame if we produce only girls.'

Alesha glimpsed his faint smile. 'Why, when their mother is a fine example of what women can achieve?'

'An attempt to soften me up for the inevitable consummation?' She was heading down a dangerous path, and she silently damned her runaway tongue.

'The chemistry we share bothers you?'

Bother was too tame a description!

'And chemistry is an automatic guarantee for satisfaction between the sheets?'

What is the matter with you? a silent voice screamed inside her head. Are you *insane*?

'Did your ex gift you that?'

She silently damned herself for metaphorically opening a vein. 'You expect me to answer such a question?'

He was silent for several seconds…seconds during which she found it difficult to hold his gaze. 'You just did.'

It would be so easy to tell him to go to hell, and she almost did. Except sanity ruled her tongue and she maintained a dignified silence. He had depth of character, a silent strength that had been lacking in Seth…although she hadn't seen it at the time.

Blinded by what she imagined to be love, Alesha decided with cynicism. Seth had played his part well…as she'd soon discovered.

This, her second wedding night, was so vastly different from that of her first wedding when she'd been surrounded by family and friends, and filled with love for her new husband and barely containing a breathless excitement for the night when she and Seth were alone.

A faint bubble of cynical amusement rose in her throat to remain unuttered.

She'd thought being in love resolved everything, except it hadn't. The magical wedding night she'd imagined didn't happen due to her new husband imbibing vintage champagne a little too freely. And the sex had been…less than she'd imagined it would be. Afterwards, when she had refused to give in to his demands that they upgrade their home and lifestyle, and allow him an unlimited expense account, the sex had become a punishment she had endeavoured to avoid…to her cost. And she'd walked away, vowing never to be taken in by another man in her lifetime.

Yet here she was, a few hours into a second marriage she didn't want to the man of her father's choice. Sharing the same room in separate beds…for how long? One night…two?

After all, in the dark of night, sex was just… sex. No big deal. Right?

So why did she feel like a cat treading hot bricks?

Because instinct warned she was way out of her depth with a man of Loukas' calibre. There was something about him, an intrinsic, almost raw sexuality that bordered on the primitive.

Intoxicating, brazen, shameless.

A part of her ached for the experience, while sanity cautioned she might not survive with her emotions intact.

It was almost a relief when Eloise entered the dining room to clear the table, and Alesha elected tea in preference to the strong espresso Loukas favoured.

How soon could she conceivably offer an excuse and retire to bed? Another hour or two? Did Loukas have anything planned?

A tiny bubble of laughter rose in her throat. *Sure*…like they'd settle comfortably in the media room and watch a movie on DVD?

Resorting to cynical humour was a defence mechanism she chose to employ against an increasing onset of nervous tension.

'I have a few international calls to make.' Loukas studied her expressive features, and it was almost as if he knew the pattern of her thoughts. 'Maybe an hour or two ahead of me on the computer as the business day begins in Europe.'

Her relief was palpable, and she only hoped it wasn't evident. 'Sure. Go for it.' She stood and moved away from the table, aware he did the same, and she preceded him from the room, then headed for the upper level.

Tomorrow she'd familiarize herself with the

house and its several levels…but for now she ascended the curved staircase and made her way along the gallery to their suite.

Her choices numbered many: a leisurely soak in the spa-bath; slipping into bed with a book— if she could locate one. Sliding between the covers of one of the two beds and attempting to sleep.

As if she'd be able to do that, when every nerve in her body would be alert and tuned into Loukas' appearance.

Two beds…would he sleep alone, or choose to share her own?

Hell. She didn't even know *which* bed was his.

What if she selected the wrong bed and he took it as an invitation to share?

Dammit, since when had she become so ambivalent?

Since her separation and divorce from Seth, she'd regained her independence, healed, and forged a reputation as a confident savvy young businesswoman who'd earned her rightful position as Dimitri Karsouli's colleague.

Very little, if anything, fazed her. Certainly not a man of any calibre…except Loukas.

She'd stayed away from him, careful not to show so much as a glimmer more than mere friendship. Aware, even from the first moment she'd met him that he was more than she could handle.

Light and dark, mesmeric…possessed of a sensual power that electrified and frightened. Because she instinctively knew he'd want it all…the heart of a woman, her body, her soul.

And she couldn't *be* that woman. Didn't want to be *absorbed* so totally that there was nothing left except him.

Now, she didn't know. So much had changed. *She* had changed.

No longer did she believe in love. At least, not the happy-ever-after enduring kind that lasted a lifetime.

Nor did she intend to place her trust in any man.

Once burned by flame, it was the height of foolishness to toy with it again.

For timeless minutes she stood taking in the superb furnishings in the spacious suite. Despite the luxurious accoutrements there was an underlying air of comfort that held appeal. The muted colours aided relaxation, and she wondered if they'd been a deliberate choice by the interior decorator responsible for creating the refurbishment.

Decisiveness had to be a plus, she perceived as she collected sleepwear and moved into the en suite where the spa-bath beckoned invitingly.

Mellow, she coveted the slow slide into the kind of relaxation that aided an easy sleep. Hopefully way before Loukas entered the room, so she wouldn't be aware of his presence until morning…and maybe not even then, if he rose early to make use of the downstairs gym.

Heaven, Alesha breathed as she sank into the warm bubbling water and positioned her head against the cushioned rest.

Ten minutes, she allowed…then she'd switch off the jets, release the water, dry off, and slip into bed.

It was almost midnight when Loukas closed down the laptop and muted the desk lamp. He'd spoken to Constantine in the Athens office, liaised with two colleagues in Paris, another in Rome. There'd been data to peruse to which he added his input, and the stock markets.

He lifted his arms and stretched, easing out the kinks in his shoulders, then he sat in contemplative silence for several long minutes before rising to his feet.

In the kitchen he filled a glass with chilled water, drank it down, then he checked the security system and moved quietly upstairs.

The master bedroom suite bore the softened light from muted lamps, and it took only a brief glance to determine both beds were empty.

A slight frown creased his forehead as he crossed to the en suite, knocked quietly, and when there was no answer he opened the door.

For a moment he stood taking in the scene...the soft pulsing jets in the spa-bath, the slender feminine form whose facial features in repose looked peaceful, almost childlike and bare of artificial enhancements.

Her soft, slightly parted mouth almost begged the touch of his own. Fine, almost porcelain skin moulded delicate bone structure, a perfect nose, and long natural eyelashes fanned out from petal-like eyelids.

He moved quietly towards the bath and switched off the jets, then he collected one of several large folded bath-towels and spoke her name.

There was no sign she heard him, and his gaze skimmed over her slender curves, the soft swell of her breasts with their tender peaks, the delicate waist, flat stomach with its slim gold pin with a strategically placed diamond attached to her navel. A cheeky jewellery accessory that winked and gleamed beneath the water's surface.

He felt the stirring of arousal, and banked it down.

'Alesha.' His voice was firm, and he caught the faint flutter of her eyelashes. 'Wake up.'

He saw the moment his words penetrated her

subconscious, the sudden upwards sweep of her lashes as she came awake, and the stark mix of startled surprise and fear in the depths of her eyes the instant before she recognized him and gained the reality of her surroundings.

'It's after midnight,' he said quietly. 'You fell asleep.'

Loukas glimpsed her attempt to control the fleeting expressions chasing her features, saw the embarrassment change to indignation as she automatically used her hands to shield the vulnerable parts of her body.

'Leave the towel and go...*please.*'

He was tempted to release the water, scoop her out and wrap her in the towel, then carry her to bed. *His.*

Except when he took her, it would be because she wanted him, not an act she conceded out of duty or mere compliance.

He might be many things, and he'd been called on several...but he stood by his word.

So he did as she requested and closed the door behind him, then he shed his clothes, took a cool shower, and slid between the sheets to lie with his arms crossed behind his head.

He watched idly as she emerged into the bedroom attired in cotton sleep trousers and a singlet top, looking impossibly young.

A slight smile widened his generous mouth as she avoided meeting his gaze, and he waited until she slipped beneath the covers before closing the lamps.

'Goodnight.' His voice was an indolent drawl in the darkness, and he only just heard her muffled response.

CHAPTER FIVE

ALESHA woke to light filtering through partly closed shutters along the wall of glass facing east.

For a brief moment she felt slightly disorientated by her unfamiliar surroundings, then memory surfaced as she cautiously examined the spacious room.

Specifically the large bed next to the one she'd occupied through the night…and she experienced a sense of relief to find it empty.

She brushed a hand through her hair and checked the time, saw it was almost eight, and hurriedly slid from the bed before gathering up fresh clothes and disappearing into the en suite to complete her morning routine and dress.

Jeans and a stylish tee sufficed, and she caught her hair in a ponytail, added gloss to her lips, then she made her way downstairs to the kitchen.

Coffee would be good, breakfast even better, and she entered the spacious, beautifully appointed kitchen to discover Eloise stacking the dishwasher, with no sign of Loukas in sight.

'Good morning.' Alesha kept it light and offered a warm smile, which the housekeeper returned in kind.

'It's a lovely day,' Eloise added. 'What can I get you for breakfast?'

'If it's okay with you, I'll make coffee, and just grab some cereal and fruit, and take it out onto the terrace.'

'I can easily prepare a cooked breakfast if you'd prefer.'

'Thanks, but cereal is fine.'

There was something infinitely relaxing in looking out over the harbour. Small and large craft sprinkled the sparkling Port Jackson waters; tugboats guided a massive tanker towards the wharves, while ferries cruised the distance between the city and Manly.

The cityscape bore tall modern high-rise buildings in varying architectural designs, their plate-glass windows glinting as the sun rose in the sky.

No matter where she'd travelled, Sydney was *home*. The place of her birth and education. It held *familiarity* for her. Memories, all of them good…until Seth. And just as she emerged whole and healed, she was flung into the unknown again by her father's hand.

'Finish your coffee, then we'll collect the rest of your belongings from the apartment.'

Loukas had the silent tread of a cat, and she replaced her cup down onto its saucer with care before she turned to meet his gaze.

Attired in jeans and a chambray shirt, he bore a deceptively casual air that was the antithesis of the man he'd proven himself to be.

It was the eyes, Alesha perceived. Dark silken depths that were too perceptive for anyone's peace of mind…especially hers.

Oh, why not admit it? He unsettled her, increasing her vulnerability to a point where she felt constantly on edge in his presence.

'I can manage to do that on my own.'

'You don't need to.'

'What if I prefer to?'

'Give it up, Alesha.'

She tilted her head and held his gaze with equanimity. 'I was unaware taking your name meant alienating my freedom of choice.'

He rested a hip against the edge of the table and leant towards her, not exactly crowding her in, but close…too close.

'You prefer the difficult route to a simple one?' He waited a beat as her eyes darkened at his proximity. 'Or do you merely enjoy debating me?'

She resembled a startled foal whenever he encroached on her personal space, and his gaze narrowed fractionally as the pulse at the base of her throat began to visibly thud.

'You lucked out if you want a subservient wife who will agree with your every word.'

'It should make for an interesting life.'

Her smile was deliberate. 'You think?'

Loukas stood to his feet. 'Collect your keys, then we'll leave. Presumably you've forgotten one of Dimitri's charitable causes is hosting an event this evening and our presence is expected?'

He glimpsed the conflicting emotions pass fleetingly across her expressive features before she managed to control them. 'I doubt you packed a suitable gown.'

She hadn't. Neither gown nor shoes, nor evening clutch.

Surely she had the event entered in her diary? Yet she'd neglected to check…understandable given her father's sudden death, the funeral, Dimitri's will. Dammit, her *marriage*.

But *tonight*? She could have put in a token appearance even with Loukas as her partner as a matter of respect. But wearing Loukas' wedding ring, how long would it take for the inevitable question to arise? The speculation?

Dear heaven, the need to maintain some form of pretence as Alesha *Andreou*?

She didn't want to go there…at least, not so *soon*. Yet she'd been raised with a strong sense of duty, a respect for bona fide charitable causes, and this evening's fundraiser was indeed a special one, fostering a terminally ill child with the opportunity to fulfil a much revered wish.

Alesha gathered her crockery and flatware together and deposited both in the kitchen before she ascended the stairs to collect her keys.

She caught sight of Loukas waiting in the foyer as she re-entered the upstairs gallery, and she ran lightly downstairs.

'I'll be a while.'

It was a parting shot, a last-ditch attempt for independence that failed miserably as he swung open one of the two solid-panelled doors and indicated the four-wheel drive parked in the driveway.

'Let's go.'

She threw him a fulminating look that had no visible effect whatsoever, and they rode the distance to Double Bay in silence.

The apartment was exactly as she'd left it, and she became extremely conscious of Loukas' presence as he overrode every objection she made.

Okay, so she'd transfer all her clothes, shoes and personal possessions. Any decision about the furniture and the apartment itself could wait. The practical side voted she maintain it as was. Logically, she should lease it out.

Except it bore her personal stamp, with everything carefully chosen to create a perfect blend of muted colours, a kitchen to die for, beautifully elegant furniture and furnishings.

Hers alone…a sanctuary representing a personal triumph through darkness to light, the re-emergence of strength and resolve.

'I'll clear the tallboy and dresser drawers while you take the wardrobe.'

She looked at him askance.

He intended to gather together her personal stuff? Lingerie, briefs, bras?

'I'll take care of those.'

Except he was already there, opening a drawer and scooping up pastel silk thongs, satin briefs, lacy bras and transferring them into a packing box.

'Must you?' she flung with exasperation, barely quelling the urge to hit him.

His husky chuckle incensed her, and she reacted without thought, aiming the shoe she held in her hand with accuracy, only to watch in stunned disbelief as he fielded it and placed it down with care.

His smile was still in place, but the expression in his dark eyes sent chills scudding the length of her spine.

'You want to play?'

Not the sort of game he had in mind, and she silently damned her foolish action. 'I don't *do* sex in the middle of the day.'

One eyebrow lifted in cynical humour. 'You prefer furtive foreplay beneath the cover of darkness?'

As Seth had? Ensuring any strike came without warning, and the advantage became his?

In the animal kingdom, she qualified, Seth was akin to a reptile—while Loukas came from an entirely different species…primitive, highly sensual, and infinitely dangerous. A very sexual man, whose reputation with women was legend.

And now he was hers.

Or more accurately…she was *his*.

Something moved in her eyes, then was quickly gone.

Loukas' gaze narrowed as he glimpsed the fine hold she had on her emotions, and how unaware she was that he could so easily read them.

Just what was it about her brief marriage that had changed her from a delightful young woman possessed of an engaging personality into someone who rarely laughed and shied away from men?

Abuse? Physical, mental…or both?

The extent of his anger at the possibility surprised him, and he banked it down as he turned his attention to the next drawer. 'Let's get this done.'

Methodical placement of clothes being her *thing* made for easy transference from wardrobe to packing boxes, and she focused on the chore at hand while attempting to ignore Loukas' presence.

Difficult, she acknowledged, when he was *there*, a physical entity that filled her with an edgy awareness and made her supremely conscious of every breath she took.

Tonight…she really didn't want to think about the evening, or how much it would cost her to play an expected part at Loukas' side. To smile, converse and *pretend*.

You'll be fine, Alesha silently assured herself as she slid the zip fastener home on an exquisite gown in deep emerald green whose off-the-shoulder design hugged her slender curves. She opted to leave her hair loose, and employed the skilful use of make-up to highlight her eyes and accent her generously moulded mouth.

Six-thirty for seven meant leaving the house at six, and she attached diamond studs to her ears, added a matching pendant on a slim gold chain, only to have the clasp prove difficult.

'Problems?' Loukas crossed to stand behind her, and she held her breath as his fingers brushed her own as he slid the clip into place.

The exclusive tones of his cologne teased her senses, and she stood still, unable in those long seconds to do anything but breathe.

He seemed to surround her, a magnetic force that caused her body to pulse, irrespective of the dictates of her brain.

For one wild moment she wondered if he knew.

Dear heaven, she hoped not.

'Ready?'

She stepped away from him and collected her evening clutch. 'Yes.'

As ready as she'd ever be, she vowed silently as the Aston Martin swept through streets slick from an early evening shower.

She'd done this before, many times. Attending various functions in the company of her parents, and partnering Dimitri after her mother's death.

So what was the big deal?

You can do this, Alesha assured herself again as Loukas slid the car to a halt adjacent the main entry of one of Sydney's prestigious hotels.

With smooth efficiency the concierge arranged valet parking, and she entered the hotel foyer at Loukas' side.

A magnificent wide staircase curved to a mezzanine level where guests were gathered in the spacious lounge adjacent the grand ballroom.

Uniformed waiters and waitresses offered canapés, champagne and orange juice.

Smile. Do the meet-and-greet thing, comment on the attendance, assure Karsouli's continued support to members of the charity committee…and refer any awkward questions to Loukas.

Simple. At least it should have been.

Except she neglected to factor in Loukas' constant company, the touch of his hand at the back of her waist, the effect his warm smile had on her equilibrium. Dammit, their projected togetherness.

It was inevitable the wide diamond-encrusted wedding ring on her left hand would eventually capture attention. Coupled as it was with the plain gold band Loukas now wore, conclusions were reached and the more emboldened requested confirmation.

The news spread, with almost comical circumspection if one was inclined towards cynical amusement.

'Darling, how wonderful happiness should evolve from such recent sadness.' Words expressed by the charity committee member were genuine, and Alesha accepted the air-kiss, the obligatory hug as others followed.

Men, captains of industry, who took the opportunity to shake Loukas' hand and offer congratulations. And women, some of whom expressed their affection a little more enthusiastically to Loukas than the occasion demanded.

Two in particular, known for their flirting skills and love of high-living.

Alesha assured herself she didn't care when the exquisite blonde melded her body close and wound her arms round Loukas' neck.

To his credit, he moved his head so the intended kiss brushed the edge of his jaw, and he summoned a faint smile as he disentangled the blonde's arms.

A sparkling laugh, the hint of a moue, then the blonde turned towards Alesha. 'Darling, he's delicious. If you hadn't snared him first…' The words trailed to a halt, with no doubt of the implication.

Darling, Alesha was sorely tempted to redress, you'd have been most welcome. Instead she offered a sweet smile, and barely managed to contain her surprise as Loukas lifted her hand and brushed his lips to her sensitive palm.

For a brief moment the room and everyone in it faded as her eyes locked with his, and the air between them seemed filled with electric tension.

Then he smiled, and curled her hand within his own. 'Fortunately, she did.'

Oh, my…*what was that*?

Playing the part, a tiny imp taunted. *And he does it so well.*

'Pity,' the blonde voiced with seeming regret. 'We could have had fun.' With a pretty wave of her hand the blonde turned and melted into the crowd.

'You can let go now,' Alesha managed quietly, attempting to pull free without success, for he merely threaded his fingers through her own. She kept her voice light and a smile in place. 'Must you?'

'Yes.'

He glimpsed sudden pain darken her eyes, then it was gone.

It was perhaps as well the ballroom doors opened and the assembled guests converged towards the three main entry points.

Their table held prominent position, and the usual speeches included gratitude for previous funding together with a plea for the guests' continuing generosity.

The drinks flowed, entertainment was provided between each of the three dinner courses, and it wasn't until coffee was served that there was the opportunity for any lengthy conversation.

A DJ set discs spinning at one end of the ballroom and provided a mix of music. A time of the evening when some of the older guests began to leave, and the younger set filled the adjoining floor-space.

'Shall we?'

Dance? With him?

She had, on a few occasions in the past. Way past, when her life had been uncomplicated and she'd viewed the future as a journey of discovery.

Following her separation from Seth, the only male she'd chosen to dance with had been her father…occasions when she'd felt protected, *safe*.

Loukas and *safe* didn't equate.

In the name of heaven, *get a grip*. She was in a room filled with people, and she was being too ridiculous for words.

'Sure, why not?' she managed simply.

Except being held by him was far from simple. Even in killer heels she was conscious of his height, his restrained strength and his sexual energy.

One hand lingered at the base of her spine, and she barely controlled a faint shivery sensation as his thumb brushed a gentle pattern over the delicate bones.

If he sought to soothe, the caress had the opposite effect, and she dug her lacquered nails into his hand in a silent plea to desist.

A fruitless exercise as he drew her close, splaying the hand at her spine to hold her there.

Worse, the DJ selected a slow, seductive number and the lights dimmed low, providing a level of intimacy that made her want to pull away from him.

She tried, without success, and everything within her coalesced and became one highly sensitized ache. It made her want something she'd thought she once held in her grasp...only to be cheated as her emotional dreams were smashed into a thousand pieces.

Please, she silently begged. I can't do this.

I want my life back...the one I carefully rebuilt for myself. No emotional ties, no room for disappointment and heartache.

'I think we've managed a sufficiently convincing display,' Alesha offered evenly, and wondered if Loukas had any idea of the effort it had cost her not to tear herself away from him.

'You've had enough?'

Enough of *what*? Being held intimately close to him? Playing pretend? Why not go for broke and include *both*, with emphasis on the former?

He sounded mildly amused, and she deliberately stood on his foot.

'I'm so sorry,' she said sweetly.

'No, you're not.' He eased her to the edge of the dance floor, then began leading the way to their table.

The 'goodnight' thing took a while, and it was a relief to leave the ballroom and descend the stairs to the hotel foyer.

The concierge summoned their car, and within minutes the Aston Martin appeared in the forecourt.

Alesha slid into the passenger seat, fastened the seat belt, then she eased her head against the cushioned rest and closed her eyes.

Home, bed. And, mercifully, a restful sleep.

Except home was no longer her apartment, and it was late, which meant Loukas probably was unlikely to run an electronic check of the world markets before heading for bed.

'Headache?'

Her eyelids lifted and she turned towards him. It would be so easy to say *yes*, and she almost did. Except honesty had her shaking her head.

The night cast the car's interior with a shadowy light, throwing his profile into stark angles.

He was something else. Sophisticated, powerful…yet beneath that persona lurked a man she found difficult to fathom. Content, apparently, to enter a loveless marriage and sire progeny sans emotional involvement.

What was it with that?

She knew all the issues. Hadn't she agreed to them? Although *agree* didn't enter the equation. Choice had weighed heavily against her.

A situation that pushed her to the edge and kept her there.

'You handled the evening well.'

His silky drawl curled round her nerve-ends and pulled them to breaking point.

'While you excelled.'

'A compliment?'

She looked at him carefully. 'Of course. What else?'

'I doubt your foot's deliberate aim was accidental.'

'Really?' Alesha managed sweetly.

Loukas smiled. She was a refreshing change from the women who formed part of his business and social entourage. Women who knew how to please and were forthcoming in offering to share his bed.

Easy pickings, he reflected without shame. Aware few, if any, had any thought beyond the advantages of his wealth, the gifts, the travel, the media attention his presence gained.

It was after midnight when he garaged the car and reset the security system.

Alesha made for the staircase, reaching their suite ahead of him, and she slipped off her heels, removed her ear-studs and reached for the clasp holding her pendant in place.

Stiff, it still refused to release, and she muttered an unladylike oath beneath her breath.

'Let me.'

She hadn't heard him enter the room, and she held her breath as his fingers brushed her nape. Within seconds he freed the recalcitrant clasp and dropped the pendant into her palm.

'Thanks.'

His eyes were dark, slumbrous, as he laid a finger beneath her chin and tilted it. 'So...thank me.'

The wayward pulse at the base of her throat began its rapid thudding beat, and her eyes flared as he lowered his head down to hers.

'Don't—'

Whatever else she meant to utter didn't find voice as his mouth took hers in a kiss that grazed her lips with sensual promise, warm, caressing with deliberate intent as he sought her response.

One hand shifted to cup her nape while the other slid to the base of her spine and he drew her in against him.

Awareness flared as he deepened the kiss, his tongue an erotic force that sent the blood sizzling through her veins, flooding her inner core with a piercing sweetness until she became lost... wanting, *needing* on some subliminal level to superimpose a different image from the cruel taunts she'd received beneath Seth's hands.

It would be so easy to close her eyes and let whatever happen...*happen*.

She felt him reach for the zip fastening on her gown, sensed the slow slide as the silk slithered down her body. All she wore was a satin thong brief, and the breath hitched in her throat as he cupped her breasts and began exploring their contours, stroking each tender peak until she became powerless against the pleasurable sigh emerging from her lips.

His mouth possessed her own...persuasive, evocative, as his hand shaped her waist, then slid low to seek her swollen clitoris.

Unbidden, she arched against him, unaware of the sensual sound she made as he skilfully brought her to climax, held her there, then he probed her silken heat in readiness for his possession.

It was the intrusion that brought her to a shuddering halt, and she froze, catapulted into a stark reality where past and present images merged and became one.

Panic born from fear lent her strength as she wrenched her mouth from his own, before she railed her fists against his shoulders in a bid to be free of him.

The air in her lungs escaped in tortuous gasps as he released her, and she could only look at him in shocked dismay.

Her lips parted, but no sound emerged, and she

hugged her arms together, emotionally bereft and unable to control the way her body began to shake.

Dear God. She wanted to run and hide, except escape wasn't the answer. *Hell*...what could she say?

Any explanation would take her to a place she didn't want to go. Yet how could she not?

Her eyes widened as Loukas lifted a hand, and she instinctively took a protective backward step...a reaction that brought his narrowed gaze.

He caught the stark fear evident before she successfully masked it, and he fought against a silent rage as he reached for his discarded jacket and placed it carefully round her shoulders.

'I'm sorry.' Her voice was little more than a whisper as she instinctively caught the edges and hugged them close, barely registering the jacket was way too large on her slender frame.

Not nearly as regretful as he felt, Loukas perceived. For more reasons than the one she presumably referred to. The ache in his groin would subside...eventually. Her issue with intimacy was something else.

It placed a different emphasis on her previous short marriage, and he silently damned the man who'd clearly mistreated her.

'I should have—' she began, only to have him

place a gentle finger over her lips to still anything further she might have uttered. *Warned you*, she finished silently, stricken with a host of ambivalent emotions, the overriding one being a mix of guilt and shame.

'Don't,' he said quietly.

She wanted to escape into the en suite, don nightwear, then slip beneath the bedcovers and summon sleep. Except her feet refused to obey the command of her brain.

'I'll go sleep in another room,' Alesha offered, and felt the light brush of his fingers over her lips.

'No.'

How much would it take to lie in a bed barely a few metres from his own, and not be vividly aware of how close she'd come to the sexual act?

To recall in intimate detail the touch of his mouth on her own, the trail of his hands, and how he'd aroused her emotions to fever pitch.

Until she'd freaked out.

Oh, dear God.

How could she have come so *close*…only to freeze like a frightened virgin?

She almost wished he'd overridden her physical protest and consummated the marriage. Then she'd have got past the dread, the fear…*hell*, the stark memory of that last night beneath Seth's vicious hands.

At the very least, she owed Loukas an explanation…

Oh, please, she derided silently. Like he wouldn't already have reached the right conclusion?

Hadn't she consulted therapists and talked the talk until she knew every angle? Every possible scenario?

She'd thought she'd conquered her fear of intimacy after Seth…but then she'd never tested it. Preferring to lead a celibate life, and refusing to date.

Tonight was the closest she'd allowed any man to come…and look how that had ended? Disaster *plus*.

Even thinking about it filled her with shame… and guilt.

Move forward.

Sure, like that would happen any time soon given her reaction just now?

She shivered beneath the warmth of his jacket, and she lifted one hand, then dropped it back to her side with an awkward gesture. 'I need to—' Escape. Move away from him and the almost electric tension filling the room before—*what*? She said something foolish? Trite?

Go, a silent voice bade. And she did, heading into her en suite without a backward glance.

She took care to close the door carefully, then she removed the jacket and laid it over a chair before crossing to the vanity.

Studiously avoiding the mirror, she removed her make-up, brushed her teeth a little too vigorously, then she pulled on sleepwear, took a deep calming breath…and re-entered the bedroom.

And found it empty.

There was a sense of relief as she crossed to the bed she'd occupied the previous night, and she slid between the sheets, dimmed the lights, then closed her eyes.

To sleep, hopefully.

Except images filled her head, past and present, merging into a scrambled mix that entered her subconscious with tortured clarity, rendering her helpless as the mental reel spun out.

CHAPTER SIX

LOUKAS dragged a hand through his damp hair and reached for a towel.

A shower had eased some of the muscular tension, but not the slow-burning anger existent, for there was a part of him that wanted to physically harm the man whose mistreatment had seeded fear in the woman he'd married.

There was a word for it. And legal redress.

The question was whether Alesha had pressed charges.

Possibly not, in a bid to avoid publicity.

His eyes narrowed as he pulled on boxers… nightwear he rarely donned. The women he'd bedded were comfortable with their nudity, as well as his own.

What in hell had Alesha's ex done to turn a confident outgoing young woman into someone who had serious issues with intimacy?

Rape…physical abuse? *Both?*

His hands clenched into tight fists at the thought of her being subjected to either.

And paused momentarily to wonder why it affected him to this degree.

Had Dimitri known of his daughter's mistreatment?

Subdued lighting greeted him as he re-entered the bedroom, and his gaze swept to the slender form beneath the covers of the bed adjacent his own.

Was she asleep…or merely contriving to give that impression?

Loukas slid between the covers of his own bed, closed the lights, then lay quietly as he reflected on his every move since their arrival home from the fundraiser.

She had kissed like an angel…and he was willing to swear her reaction to his touch had been genuine.

Until she had panicked and fought against him with a desperation born of fear. Hardly the action of someone who'd sought counselling and emerged whole.

It was a while before he slept, and he came sharply awake at a soft beeping sound that had him reaching for the security sensor unit.

The glass door leading onto the terrace was unsecured, and the heat sensor detected a human form occupying a chair.

He moved quietly to his feet, checked the adjoining bed and discovered it empty.

The luminous dial on his watch showed it was several minutes past three.

Alesha? It had to be, and he extracted jeans and pulled them on, then added a tee shirt, before going in search of her.

With sure movements he crossed the gallery and ran lightly downstairs.

Subtle garden illumination provided sufficient light for him to see the slight feminine form curled up on one of four cushioned cane sofas nestled around a glass-topped table.

He made a point of ensuring she heard his approach, and he caught the quick movement of her hands as she brushed each cheek before turning towards him.

Tears?

Somehow the thought of her needing to retreat out here to cry alone touched a place in his heart he'd previously considered beyond reach.

The night air held a faint chill, and he sank down onto the sofa beside her.

'Unable to sleep?' He kept his voice light, and caught the slight shake of her head.

'I didn't mean to wake you.'

'The security sensor,' Loukas corrected. 'It beeped an alert when you opened the external door.'

His features were shadowed in the half-light, and in the distance the city breathed life with its coloured neon billboards, street-lighting…casting a dappled reflection over the dark inner harbour waters.

In a few hours the indigo sky would begin to lighten as dawn emerged, providing colour and substance to the new day.

'It's peaceful out here,' Alesha offered, aware her voice was edged with tiredness. Hardly surprising since she hadn't slept at all. Yet she didn't feel inclined to move.

Nor did she particularly want to converse. The silence of the night, the solitude it offered, acted as a soothing balm, and most of all she simply wanted to close her eyes and let it wash over her, cleanse a little and ease the ache deep inside.

There was a psychological process she needed to travel, a series of steps that would lead her from the dark back into the light, and it was better she took them alone. Then she could sleep.

'Go back to bed,' she said quietly. 'I'm fine.'

Sure she was.

'Please.'

It was the *please* that reached him, but he merely looked at her. 'I'm not going anywhere.'

Okay, so she'd pretend he wasn't there.

Difficult, when his presence acted as a compelling entity impossible to ignore. He radiated innate strength and vitality...a dramatic mesh, even in repose, that made her incredibly aware of him.

Fool, she denounced in silent self-castigation. Why...*why* did you go into orbit, when you'd mentally conditioned yourself to have sex with him?

Now you've created a wedge...oh, call it as it is...an emotional physical *chasm* so deep and wide, it'll be almost impossible to breach.

There was a part of her that felt inclined to urge him to take her to bed and...just *do* it.

Sure. Like he was going to risk her freaking out again? What man would be willing to risk rejection after being so convincingly repelled?

How could she explain that as much as she'd wanted his possession...somehow at the crucial moment Seth's angry image had superimposed Loukas' own.

'Did your ex rape you?'

His voice was quiet, steady...yet she flinched from the words, and it took a few long moments to gather herself together.

'Rape conjures up a picture involving violence.'

Loukas took hold of her hand and threaded his fingers loosely through her own. 'Sex between consenting adults should be consensual. Not a demand or used as a punishment.'

The shadows helped. His closeness provided security. And he deserved to know some of it. All of it, eventually, but for now some of it would be enough.

'Seth played a convincing part,' she began quietly. 'He fooled me, but not my father, who was against the marriage from the start.' She couldn't look at him. 'It began almost as soon as we were married, with insults at first—about my lack of spine in demanding a substantial salary package, perks. When I refused to comply, he became…rough.'

Loukas kept his voice even, in spite of the anger building inside him. 'He hit you.'

'Yes.'

'More?'

'Some,' she admitted, and heard the breath hiss between his teeth.

That any man could hurt her…dammit, *harm* her physically and emotionally enraged him. Yet if he showed any sign of it, she'd retreat even further behind the barrier she'd erected in self-protection.

She needed time to trust him, and he could give her that…even if it killed him to do so.

Meanwhile, it wouldn't be difficult to discover

the date of her first marriage, and uncover any hospital records...if any of her injuries had required hospital attention.

It became a matter of importance he discover as much as he could about what had transpired during her brief marriage. Better that, than push her for details she was reluctant to share.

For how else could he help resolve her issue with intimacy without all of the facts?

'If it's okay with you,' Alesha managed quietly, 'I'd prefer not to go into it any more tonight.'

This morning, he amended.

So where did they go from here?

With extreme care on his part.

The immediate agenda had to be a return to bed.

Soon the sky would begin to lighten, the birdlife stir and twitter with sound, and car engines would herald workers begin their trek to commence an early shift.

Dawn's break would bring men and women out for their early morning run, and the day would begin.

Sunday indicated recreation and relaxation for some. The beach, time spent cruising the inner harbour waters, following cultural pursuits, entertaining guests, sporting activities.

Maybe she'd give Lacey a call and suggest they

share part of the day together. Shop a little, linger over a latte at one of their favoured cafés.

There was pleasure in the thought, and a sense of encroaching drowsiness…something she fought, unaware of Loukas' thoughtful gaze as her eyelids slowly drifted down.

For several long minutes he viewed her softened features, noted her even breathing, then he rose quietly to his feet and carefully lifted her into his arms.

She didn't stir, and he carried her easily into the house, reset security, then he took her upstairs to their room.

He breathed in the clean smell of her hair combined with the soft drift of her perfume, and tamped down the stirring of desire.

Feelings he hadn't expected to experience, born from an emotion he consciously chose not to explore.

The covers were thrown back on the bed Alesha had occupied, and she uttered a faint protest as he relinquished his hold.

With easy economical movements he shed his jeans, tee shirt, snapped off the bed-lamp and slid into bed beside her.

With extreme care he enfolded her slender body close in against him, felt her stir, and he soothed a hand over her hair…again and again, until a soft sigh emerged from her throat and she relaxed against him in sleep, her cheek resting into the curve of his shoulder.

He could offer her safety, and hold her through the night. Be there for her, and help soothe her fears.

Of the many social functions Alesha had attended in the past, tonight's fundraiser took precedence, and was one in which she maintained a personal interest.

Children who'd suffered abuse at the hands of those who professed to love them. Adults, whose trust they deserved, yet failed to receive. The varying shades of grey to the deepest black, covering circumstances too grim for the average person to comprehend.

Tonight a few children's plight would be highlighted in order to touch the guests' hearts and persuade them to give generously.

Alesha chose a black bandage-design gown that hugged her slender curves and showcased delicate-textured skin. She confined jewellery to a slender gold necklace with matching ear-studs and bracelet, and black killer heels completed the outfit.

Minimum make-up, with emphasis on her eyes, she opted to leave her hair loose in a soft feminine style.

The event drew a pleasing number of guests,

and she stood at Loukas' side sipping champagne, acutely aware of his close proximity.

He portrayed the man he was…sophisticated, urbane, highly intelligent, successful. And he wore the verbal labels with ease, comfortable in his own skin with little, if anything, to prove.

And he was hers.

Well, not in the truest sense…yet. She bore his name, wore his ring, and she…liked him.

Admit it, you find him stunningly attractive. Sexy…incredibly sexy, she amended. And there was a part of her that craved the intimacy she instinctively rejected.

So why did she feel as if she were treading eggshells, aware she consciously watched everything she said, every action, in case it was misconstrued.

At work, home, and on social occasions such as this when she played the part of recently married *happy* wife.

A young woman who, by all accounts, should be ecstatic to be bedding one of the most eligible men on planet earth.

'Penny for them?'

She tilted her head and gifted him a teasing smile. 'Not for sharing, at any price.'

Loukas' mouth curved a little, and the hand resting at the base of her spine brushed a light trail up her back to linger at the lower edge of her nape.

Sensation spiralled through her body, and it took conscious effort to hold his dark gaze.

Dear heaven, she was almost flirting with him…for real. Not the best idea, given the tenuous quality of their relationship.

Yet it was fun, almost *safe*. Although was it? If you played with fire, you tended to get burnt.

So chill, and don't risk conflagration.

Their table was well placed, the company stimulating, and the food delectable.

The speeches held a poignancy that speared her heart, and her eyes clouded…for she could envisage so much more than the mere words conveyed. At one point her fingers tightened into a fist, and her lacquered nails dug into her palm. No one should be a victim of abuse…dear heaven, especially never a child.

Almost as if he sensed her torment, Loukas placed his hand over hers until she released her grip. His silent presence and strength comforted her and she gave him a tentative smile and returned his hold on her hand, suddenly glad he was there with her this evening.

The entertainment for the night comprised a designer fashion showing, with elegant models parading the catwalk, followed by an auction of the garments with a generous percentage gifted to the charity.

It lightened the evening, with the auctioneer really getting into the swing of it, encouraging bidders to raise the stakes.

One gown caught Alesha's interest, a deep red silk with spaghetti straps attached to a beautiful ruched bodice and a soft floor-length tiered skirt.

Loukas indicated his bid, and escalated it by increments until it reached an exorbitant amount and the one remaining bidder pulled out.

Alesha leaned towards him and said in a subdued but scandalized voice, 'Are you crazy?'

'It's a worthy cause.' His voice held a teasing indolence as he brushed his lips to her temple. 'And the gown is perfect for you.'

Oh, my. For an instant the room and everyone in it faded into nothing as his eyes locked with her own, and something violently sweet coursed through her body.

His mouth curved into an easy smile, almost as if he knew.

'Thanks.' On impulse she pressed her lips to his cheek…at least that was her intention, except he moved and her mouth met his own, and a light kiss became something else as he savoured her briefly before lifting his head.

Colour filled her cheeks, and he trailed light

fingers over the soft heat, then skimmed over one shoulder to rest at the edge of her waist.

'Dear Alesha,' a light feminine voice intruded. 'So nice to see you happy in your new marriage.'

Recovery was swift as she summoned a smile and turned towards the woman who'd stopped by to offer congratulations, only to have her heart sink.

Nicolette de Silva had a reputation for lacking tact. Even the kindest amongst her coterie of friends admitted Nicolette didn't *think* before she opened her mouth.

'Her brief liaison with that terrible man was a disaster,' Nicolette confided to Loukas. 'But then, of course, you know about that?'

'Naturally.' His voice was smooth as silk. Sufficiently so that most people would immediately cease pursuing the subject and move on.

'There were rumours, some of them extreme.' Nicolette offered a conciliatory smile. 'I believe Seth Armitage tried to sell his side of the story to the media, but nothing came of it, isn't that right, Alesha?'

Alesha's fingers clenched beneath the cover of the tablecloth, and she tensed as Loukas again took her hand in his and traced soothing fingers across the pulsing veins at her wrist.

Support? Whatever, it felt…pleasant, comforting.

A double whammy, she admitted silently as the action increased her pulse-beat and made her increasingly aware of him.

She tried to tell herself she was immune to gossip. Three years on she'd heard it all…first and second-hand. The inquisitive comments she chose not to concede or deny. The false expressions of sympathy. Each a quest for information she refused to give.

'There's no point in rehashing old history,' she managed quietly. 'Don't you agree?'

Nicolette looked momentarily distraught. 'I'm so sorry. I didn't mean to upset you.'

The weird thing was she meant it.

'Apology accepted.'

'Please do enjoy the rest of the evening.'

'We shall.'

'Red will look stunning on you.'

'Thank you.' Inherent poise enabled her to conduct a perfectly sincere conversation with one of the women sharing the table. 'It's a gorgeous gown.'

'Everyone bid. The fundraiser has proven to be an enormous success.'

'Yes, it has.'

'My condolences for the sad loss of your father. He was a wonderful man.'

It was easy to agree, and Alesha turned to offer

Loukas a slow sweet smile. 'Coffee, darling? The waiters are circling the tables as we speak.'

She was something else, Loukas perceived. Brave when it mattered, yet so hauntingly vulnerable on occasion.

Was he the only one who glimpsed what lay beneath the protective façade she'd created?

It was almost midnight when the evening came to an end, and guests began making their way into the foyer. Air-kisses were exchanged, invitations issued and the need for diary dates to be checked and acceptances confirmed.

The concierge ordered cars to be fetched with military precision, and Alesha experienced a sense of relief as the Aston Martin appeared at the hotel entrance.

Home...not exactly *home*, but the place she shared with Loukas seemed almost welcome. Even better was the prospect of shedding her clothes and slipping into bed to sleep.

If she could just erase the vivid images portrayed on screen during the evening. If she had been alone in her apartment, she would have watched a DVD and lost herself in a light comedy until sheer tiredness forced her into bed.

Except she was no longer alone.

There was a part of her that wanted to become lost in the seductive touch of a man. To be held close and feel the trail of his lips as he explored her body. Experience the joy of intimacy without the fear of cruelty.

Not just any man...Loukas.

If she'd wanted an affair to expunge unwanted memories, she would have sought one by now.

Dammit, what was she waiting for?

Love?

Oh, *please*. The emotion only existed for such a brief period of time in the real world... didn't it?

The kind that changed lives and lasted a lifetime, one man for one woman, twin souls meant only for each other...that was a beautiful fantasy with little basis in reality.

Since when had she become so cynical?

A hollow laugh rose and died in her throat, for she could pinpoint the date, the time almost to the minute.

The car turned off the New South Head Road into Point Piper, and reached the magnificent set of gates guarding the entrance to Loukas' mansion.

A modem released the gates and simultaneously lit the curved driveway as he eased the Aston Martin towards the garage.

A sense of restlessness invaded her body as she ascended the stairs...a feeling she attempted to dismiss without much success on entering the master suite.

She became extremely conscious of Loukas' presence as he shed his jacket, then loosened his bow tie.

Smooth easy movements that were uncontrived as he moved to free the buttons on his dress shirt…and she focused on discarding her evening shoes, her jewellery.

All the time she was acutely aware of him…the faint thud as he removed his shoes; the almost un-detectable slide of a zip fastening and the soft slither of material as he freed trousers.

The image of his tall, near-naked frame was hauntingly vivid. Hell, she had no problem visu-alizing the impressive breadth of his shoulders, the superb musculature tapering to a sculptured waist and lean hips.

Would there ever be a time when she could feel sufficiently confident to seduce him? Boldly explore and tease until he groaned beneath her touch?

To have him reach for her in the night and gift him the freedom of her body…to exult in untold pleasure?

She drew in a ragged breath, then released it slowly. Oh, for heaven's sake…*stop*.

Get rid of the dress, gather up your sleepwear,

escape to your en suite, remove make-up, brush teeth, fix hair into a ponytail…then go to bed.

She did all that and re-entered the bedroom to find Loukas stretched comfortably beneath the covers, arms crossed pillowing his head.

'Goodnight.' Her voice sounded slightly strangled even to her own ears as she slid between the sheets and he doused the lights.

'Sleep well.'

As if that were going to happen any time soon.

Perhaps if she lay perfectly still and conjured only pleasant thoughts…

Except nothing helped, and her thoughts assumed a kaleidoscopic mix that subdued the colours and brought Seth's image into stark black and white focus.

Go away. A silent entreaty, harsh only in her mind, had no effect whatsoever.

There was a need to remain awake, for at least then she retained a measure of control. If she slid into sleep all control would be lost and his image would emerge to haunt her as it had too frequently in the past.

She needed to win…she *had* to.

Yet slipping from her bed and joining Loukas in his took more courage than she possessed, for what if he mistook her for a former flame…or, worse, he rejected her?

So much for that plan.

Afterwards Alesha had no memory of when her subconscious led unerringly into the familiar nightmare. She only knew she was fighting to escape…crying out as she shielded her face from the stinging slaps, the harsh bite of cruel hands pinning her down, the sound of her name on his lips.

Then she came sharply awake to a room flooded with light…a room different from the one she'd occupied in her mind, and the man leaning close to her wasn't Seth.

It took one brief horrifying moment to shake free of the starkly intrusive images, and she was barely conscious of the concern evident in the dark eyes of the man watching the range of fleeting emotions chase her expressive features before she gained the control to mask them.

Loukas lifted a hand, saw her eyes flare with sudden fear, and swallowed the curse that rose to his lips as he smoothed a wayward lock of hair behind her ear, then let his hand trail along her jaw to cup her chin and press a thumb to her quivering mouth.

There seemed no past, only the present, and words fell from her lips without conscious thought. 'Please…'

She looked stricken as the realization of what

she said sank in, and she lifted her hands in a defensive gesture as he dispensed with them and drew her close.

His skin was warm against her cheek, and she felt a hand cradle her head as the other slid low over the back of her waist.

It felt good...*he* felt good, and she breathed in the scent of him, the faint traces of soap, cologne and the muskiness of man.

His hand brushed a path over her spine, rested briefly at her nape, then slid slowly down in a slow soothing pattern that did much to settle her ragged breathing.

She didn't want to move, and she instinctively lifted her arms to link her hands together at the back of his neck.

He grazed his lips over her cheek, nuzzled her ear, then eased his mouth down to savour the curve at the base of her neck...and sensed the breath hitch in her throat.

A hand shifted to her waist and gently slipped beneath the sleep top to skim the warm skin as he traced a path to her breast, cupped it, then brushed the tender peak until it swelled to his touch.

With care, he deepened the kiss, tasting, exploring the inner texture, the sensitive tissues as he encouraged her response. Her body jerked as he took her lower lip into his mouth and bit down gently, and she moved restlessly in his arms, seeking more, *wanting* so much more.

With care he eased the cotton top high, and when she didn't resist he removed it completely.

'Beautiful,' Loukas said gently as he shaped each breast, then soothed their softness before lowering his head to caress one tender peak as it hardened into a swollen bead that begged to be suckled.

Her body arched against his own, and she cried out as he took the peak into his mouth and used the edge of his teeth to heighten her pleasure.

There was satisfaction as her hands began their own discovery, shaping his shoulders, sliding slowly down the bunched muscles to his forearms, before moving to his ribs, where, once there, she trailed light fingers over his chest, toyed with the tight buds, then slipped to frame his waist.

His breath caught as she leaned in and placed her lips over one tight bud…and drew it between her teeth, only to release it and trail a path to his navel, explored a little, and sighed when he pulled her down onto the bed and took her mouth with his own.

Frankly sensual, he plundered at will, hungry, almost demanding as she matched him in a primitive oral dance where she became lost…totally lost in the magic he evoked.

There was no sense of time or place…only the man, and she whimpered in protest as he began easing back, softening his touch until his mouth drifted gently over her own, then he lifted his head and regarded her carefully.

Alesha had no coherent thought as her emotions went into meltdown.

Dear God, what had just happened here?

She couldn't tear her eyes away from his, almost as if she were held captive by the smouldering heat…the intense passion, unrestrained and primitive in that instant. And the control, leashed, but easily broken by a careless word or gesture on her part.

'Your call.'

CHAPTER SEVEN

HE COULD come so close, yet stop if she asked him to?

How could he do that? Ohmigod…how could *she*?

'Please.' The word whispered from Alesha's lips, a fragile sound barely lucid in the stillness of the night.

His eyes were dark…so dark, she became lost in their depths as he brushed a thumb-pad gently over her lower lip.

'Do you know what you're asking?'

She did, on some subliminal level. Yet she couldn't stop, for it was as if she were being driven by an inner force that left her powerless.

'Yes.' As proof she sought his mouth with her own, and held on as he took possession in a kiss that made her forget everything except his touch, the hunger…and the innate knowledge she didn't want him to stop.

With care he eased off her sleep trousers, taking his time as he trailed gentle fingers over the surface of her skin, then he cupped one ankle and lowered his head down to brush his lips over the delicate arch.

Slow, he wanted slow and easy, building the tension, stoking the passion until he filled her sensual world.

It became a voyage of discovery, learning what caused her breath to hitch, the pleasurable sigh as he explored her breasts, savoured the sensitive curve at the edge of her neck…the way her body arched when he palmed the highly sensitive place between her thighs.

He felt the faint sting of her nails as her fingers bit into his shoulders, and he reciprocated with a teasing bite to the soft underside of one breast.

Naked, he saw her eyes widen as her hand brushed his arousal, and he glimpsed her brief panic, then it was gone as he took possession of her mouth in an erotic kiss that brought a purr of pleasure.

It was then he trailed his mouth in a slow caress down her throat, felt the slight vibration as he lingered there before he began grazing a sensual tasting towards her navel, circled his tongue round the diamond pin, then traced an evocative path to the intimate folds guarding her sensitive clitoris.

He felt her tense, then utter a faint sob as he bestowed the most intimate kiss of all, taking infinite care as her tension built, urging her high until she reached the brink…then he held as she fell.

And glimpsed the tears well in her eyes, the soundless movement of her lips as she struggled to find the words, and he trailed gentle fingers over each cheek, dispensing the warm moisture.

It was more, so much more than she believed it possible to experience, and she cradled his face and urged it towards her own as she sought his mouth in a kiss so expressive there was no need for words.

She felt mesmerized by the darkness in his eyes, the passion clearly evident as he moved over her, and she managed a strangled plea to turn off the light. Only to have him shake his head.

How could she explain that in the darkness she hadn't had to witness the hatred of the man who'd only married her for material gain? A man who had used sex as a punishment.

'Loukas—'

'Open your eyes,' he chided gently. 'I want you to see me, only me, and know who and what I am, and the pleasure I can give you.'

'Please. I—'

'Trust me, *agape mou*.' His mouth closed on

her own as he positioned his length and eased in, careful to ensure she could accommodate him before filling her completely.

At first he didn't move, almost as if he sensed she needed to absorb his possession, and her eyes widened as he shifted his weight and began to withdraw, only to increase the pace as her vaginal muscles caught his rhythm and matched it, until he took her high…so high she could only cling to him and experience the ride.

She felt alive. Acutely sensitive to every nerve in her body. This…*this* was how it was meant to be.

Not just sex…something so much more.

Body, mind, and spirit coalesced into one entity to provide a sensual magic.

Electrifying, primitive, exquisite.

She wanted to thank him, except she couldn't find the words for what she wanted to say.

Instead she lifted a shaky hand and placed it against his cheek, then brushed his mouth with her own.

She expected him to withdraw, and she gasped as he caught her close and rolled onto his back, taking her with him.

A slow smile curved his lips as he eased her into a sitting position astride him, and he took in her pink cheeks, the gleaming brown eyes dreamy with lingering passion. The softly parted mouth swollen from his kisses, the tousled hair framing her face.

His hands clasped her waist, and he used each thumb to trace a light pattern over her stomach…and felt her quiver beneath his touch.

This is the aftermath? Alesha mused as she felt him swell inside her. A spiral of sensation curled deep within and rose through her body… sensuous, consuming, *witching*.

His eyes held hers, and she was unable to look away as he began to move, taking her with him as she held on and joined him in a ride that held her spellbound with intense pulsating pleasure.

It was almost more than she could bear, and he drew her trembling body close and pressed his lips to her temple.

He murmured words she didn't quite catch as he nestled her head into the curve of his shoulder, and she lay there, too emotionally spent to move.

She must have slept, for she became aware of a warm body close to her own and the drift of fingers trailing a light path over the slender curve of her waist.

Her eyes flew open, and for one agonizing second her body tensed…then she recognized the bed, the room, the man who held her.

She lay perfectly still as memory of the night filled her mind, and she swallowed the sudden lump that rose in her throat.

'Look at me,' Loukas commanded gently, and when she did he captured her chin, giving her little option but to hold his dark gaze.

Her mouth quivered, and he brushed the pad of his thumb over its sensitive fullness.

'What do you want from me?'

'Whatever you choose to give.'

It wasn't the answer she expected. 'Last night—'

'Was beautiful,' he completed, and saw the soft pink colour her cheeks.

It had been all about her…her pleasure, her orgasm. What would he say if she told him it was her first?

A sudden thought swept her eyes wide. Ohmigod…he couldn't know, surely? She'd been blind with ecstasy, totally out of herself. Had she cried? Please, dear heaven, she didn't scream?

Was this where they conducted a post-coital report?

Should she thank him?

For what?

A miraculous melting of her frozen emotions? Like one sexual encounter would do it?

Staying here quiescent was madness. He'd take

it as an invitation for *more*, and, besides, daylight filtered through the shutters.

His hand slid to her stomach…her *bare* stomach. A touch that made her aware she wore nothing beneath the bedcovers, and she shifted as he traced her ribcage, only to pause as he encountered a small hard lump on one rib, followed by another.

Alesha uttered a distressed sound as Loukas discovered the scar lesion beneath her breast, the legacy of a vicious bite.

'Don't.' Except she was too late to prevent Loukas from peeling back the bedcovers, and any move she made to escape from the bed was easily stalled.

'Are these *it*?' Loukas demanded in a danger-ously soft voice. 'Or are there more?'

More. Cracked ribs, long healed.

Her eyes met his, hardening to obsidian shards. Anger rose from the deep well in which she'd buried it. She drew in a shuddering breath. 'Let me go.'

And let her escape to curl into a foetal ball alone? 'No.'

Only her father knew she'd summoned a lawyer from a hospital bed and filed for divorce. And paid Seth to get out of her life so she could rebuild her own.

'You want me to admit I was a blind fool and should have listened to my parents' caution?' She was like a runaway train, unable to stop. 'That I should have realized much sooner that it was the Karsouli wealth he wanted...not me, and that the entire engagement and lead-up to the marriage had simply been an act?'

Loukas wrapped his arms around her slender form and drew her in against him, sheltering her even as anger against the man who'd hurt her consumed him. To think of her as the victim of one man's uncontrollable rage almost undid him.

A shiver shook her slender frame as she felt his muscles tense. 'Please.' She couldn't remain where she was, naked and vulnerable.

'Stay,' he said gently.

What of her own emotions? He'd awakened something inside her she hadn't known existed. Feelings that tugged her heartstrings and made her think of the impossible.

And that would never do.

She'd given her heart once, only to have that love blow up in her face. There was no way she'd risk gifting her heart again.

Yet it felt good to be held curved in against him. His warmth surrounded her, the beat of his heart solid and even against her back. His arms offered a protective haven, and on an early Sunday morning there was no need to rise, shine and prepare for a day in the city.

* * *

Alesha spent the morning at her apartment, checked with Reception for any mail, made a few phone calls, one of which enlisted the continued services of her cleaning lady…another to Lacey suggesting they spend the afternoon at Darling Harbour.

The day was cool, the skies grey with the threat of showers, and she chose to don designer jeans, a tee shirt over which she pulled on a thigh-length knitted jacket, and she fixed a belt low on her hips. Knee-length boots completed the outfit.

By chance she found a convenient parking space not too far distant from where she'd arranged to meet Lacey, and after exchanging an affectionate hug they made for a nearby café and ordered lattes.

'So,' Lacey began. *'Tell.'*

Alesha lifted an eyebrow. 'As in?'

'This is Lacey, best friend, confidante… remember? I have your happiness at heart.' The look she offered held thoughtful concern as she queried quietly, 'Are you?'

Prevarication wouldn't work. Lacey would see through it in a second. 'Happy? It's early days.'

'Yes, I guess it is. So…moving right along?'

The benefit of friendship was being in tune, and they were, instinctively aware when to pause or pursue a subject.

'Let's focus on you.' Alesha took an appreciative sip of her latte.

'Too boring.'

'Elucidate. Life, John, work?'

'He wants the ring, house in the burbs, kids.'

'And you don't?'

'I've known him for ever. We fit together well. But I want more than just…contentment. Warm and fuzzy is fine twenty or more years down the track. But now?'

'Try adding some excitement.'

'Did that, and all I got was the *look*. You know the one…like have I suddenly flipped?'

'I'm almost afraid to ask.'

Lacey leaned in close to confide, and a few minutes later Alesha didn't know whether to roll her eyes or laugh. 'Subtle—not.'

Afterwards they wandered the various shops, boutiques and stalls, sharing company with an eclectic mix of people. Girls sporting boho chic, guys dressed from top to toe in black; a television personality with his wife and children; tourists. As well as the social set enjoying a late leisurely lunch in the restaurants overlooking the inner harbour.

Dusk was encroaching as Alesha headed towards Point Piper, and her pulse quickened to a faster beat as she garaged the car.

Loukas' black Aston Martin was parked in its customary bay, and she entered the foyer, then headed for the staircase.

There was a need to shower and change before dinner, and she walked into the master suite, only to pause at the sight of Loukas in the process of shedding his clothes.

Fluid muscles moved and flexed beneath smooth olive skin…superb musculature honed to a peak of physical fitness.

Heat unfurled deep inside her with the memory of what they'd shared during the night. How his mouth had devoured her…the touch of his hands, the movement of his body within her own. Oh, dear God, the sweet ecstasy he created within as he played her with unhurried grace, urging her high until she shattered in his arms.

There was a part of her that wanted to cross the room, lean in close and lift her mouth to his and seek the wickedly sensual slide of his tongue as it explored, tantalized…and possessed.

At that moment he turned, and dark eyes speared her own as a smile curved his generously moulded mouth.

'How was your afternoon with Lacey?'

'Great.' She consciously swallowed as he freed the zip fastening on his trousers and dispatched them. 'We explored Darling Harbour.'

What was she *doing* standing here watching him undress like a fascinated voyeur?

An impertinent imp silently taunted, *Because he's well worth the look.*

Alesha turned away, suddenly cross with herself, and she tugged off her boots, freed the belt and discarded her woollen jacket.

She heard the faint buzz of an electric shaver and relaxed a little. If she moved quickly, she'd be able to shed her jeans and tee and reach her own en suite before Loukas finished shaving.

Minutes later she activated the shower, shed bra and briefs, then she stepped into the large marble-tiled cubicle, caught up soap and began sliding the scented tablet over her body.

Her skin felt sensitive, *alive*, in a way it never had before, and each movement of the soap brought a vivid reminder of his touch. If she closed her eyes, she could almost believe he was *there*.

To have her every waking thought filled with his image after one night in his bed was crazy. Yet try as she might she couldn't shake him from her mind.

A faint groan emerged from her throat minutes later as she closed the water dial and caught up a towel.

Don't think…in the name of heaven don't let your mind slip back and compare the past with the present.

Yet how could she not?

Sex with Loukas had been mind-blowing. Except it hadn't just been sex, it had been *intimacy*, at a level she hadn't previously experienced.

A shaft of sheer sensation spiralled through her body at the mere thought…

Oh, *move right along*, why don't you? Focus on the prosaic. Get dressed, go join Loukas for dinner, indulge in pleasant conversation…and escape in due course with the need for an early night.

Rethink that excuse, or he might take it as an invitation to join her in bed. Time spent on her laptop, catching up with email, work…that should do it.

Act…you're good at it, she admonished as she forked delicious morsels from her plate.

Did Loukas guess she was harbouring a conflicting mess of nerves? Possibly. He was an intelligent man, and way too astute for her peace of mind.

Why should she feel so acutely sensitive…on edge, and extremely conscious of him? Dammit, she could still *feel* him inside her, his penetration so deep and all-consuming her vaginal muscles quivered on mere reflection.

Oh, hell. Now she was *really* losing it.

Somehow she managed to get through dinner, and when she was done she excused herself on the pretext of work.

Loukas let her go, his gaze thoughtful as he watched her leave the room. She was like a cat treading hot bricks, at odds with herself, *him*.

He tamped down the inclination to go after her. Instead, he refilled his cup with coffee, then took it into his home office and participated in a conference call with the Andreou Athens office, issued orders, and faced the possibility he might need to personally deal with the problem.

It was late when Alesha closed the laptop down and headed towards the master suite, only to find it empty.

She completed her nightly routine, discarded clothes for sleep trousers and top, then she stood hesitantly unsure whether to occupy Loukas' bed or her own.

There was a part of her that wanted the comfort of his arms, his body and the pleasure he could gift her.

'One or the other,' Loukas declared from the doorway, startling her. 'But we share.'

She turned and offered him a level look. 'What if I choose not to?'

'We sleep together,' he drawled. 'With the emphasis on sleep.' He pulled his shirt free, tended to the buttons and reached for the zip fastening on his trousers, shed them and crossed to his en suite.

Alesha slid into bed, her own, closed her eyes and pretended to sleep, only to unconsciously tense as she sensed the bedcovers shift and Loukas joined her in bed.

'Sleep well, *agape mou.*'

His voice held quiet amusement, and she refrained from uttering a word in response.

Within minutes his breathing steadied, and she silently cursed his ability to fall asleep so easily.

At some stage she must have succumbed, for she woke at dawn feeling warm, secure…and aware she lay gathered in against a hard male body.

Had she moved in the night…or had he?

Did it matter?

The question was how she could extricate herself without waking him. A mission in itself, given his arm lay heavy across her waist.

It was a nice feeling.

Nice? Oh, please. The word didn't even begin to cut it. It felt so good, so *right*, there was a part of her that wanted to remain where she was, curled in against him.

Safe, secure, *here* where she was meant to be.

Where she wanted to be.

To touch him, lightly, with her lips, the tips of her fingers…to watch him stir, become aware, awake. And see his mouth curve into that sensual smile he did so well, the soft gleam appear in those dark eyes…and have his mouth close over hers in the prerequisite that would lead to early-morning sex.

Whoa. What was happening here?

Being held in his arms was one thing…sex, a whole different ball game. One she didn't feel sufficiently equipped to play. At least, not yet. But just for a moment, while he slept, she savoured the luxury and let her mind wander to possible maybes…until reality surfaced.

So, just shift his arm, and move. What's the big deal?

But what if…? Oh, hell.

'I can almost hear your mind working.'

So much for thinking he still slept.

'Then you'll know I want out of this bed.'

She was almost certain she sensed his soft laugh. 'I can't persuade you to stay?'

'No.'

'Pity.' He removed his arm and rolled onto his back as she escaped from the bed, taking pleasure in watching her cross the room.

A beautiful young woman, who came alive beneath his touch, wondrous at the measure of her response, yet tentative about losing her inhibitions.

There was a part of him that wanted the opportunity to physically thrash the man who'd treated her with such deliberate mercilessness.

Except there was a better, more subtle way to inflict pain. He had the resources, the influence, the knowledge.

All he needed to do was set the wheels in motion.

CHAPTER EIGHT

PEAK-HOUR traffic into the city seemed more hectic and hazardous than usual, and Alesha silently cursed her independence in refusing to ride in to the office earlier with Loukas.

It set the day on a wrong foot; her laptop refused to boot up, her PA called in sick, and almost anything that could go wrong…did.

Worse, her BMW developed a puncture en route home at day's end and the spare happened to be flat. Enlisting the help of an automobile service took wait time, together with the need to have the car towed to an approved workshop, where she called for a taxi to take her home.

Loukas arrived as she paid off the driver, and she grimaced a little.

'Don't ask,' Alesha declared as he reached her side. 'You really don't want to know.'

He examined her pale features, the tenseness apparent as he cupped her chin and tilted it. 'You weren't in an accident?'

Her eyes met his with fearless disregard. 'No.' Without preamble she relayed the puncture, the flat spare.

'You should have called me.'

It simply hadn't occurred to her to do so. 'Why? I took care of it.'

He touched a light finger to her lower lip. 'Next time, call.'

He'd been concerned about her?

'Maybe.'

'Do it, Alesha.'

He cared? Really cared enough to worry about her safety? No other man, with the exception of her father, had shown such concern.

Loukas managed to surprise her, when she least expected it, and whatever frustration the day held dissipated to nothing.

'Okay, I will. I promise.'

Standing so close to him was beginning to affect her, and she moved around him, entered the foyer and ran lightly upstairs.

She thought wistfully of the spa-bath, a scented candle or three, and muted soothing music. Except it wasn't going to happen. Instead she'd settle for a leisurely shower.

On reaching the master suite she discarded her outer clothes and entered the en suite, loosened her hair, set the water dial to medium, then she shed bra and briefs and stepped into the large tiled stall.

Heaven, she determined as the water cascaded over her body, and she reached for shampoo, lathered her hair, rinsed and applied conditioner, then she reached for the scented soap…only to freeze as the glass door opened and Loukas joined her.

Splendidly naked…as if he'd be *clothed*, a wicked imp taunted…he loomed large in the confines of the shower stall.

Shocked surprise didn't cover it. Without conscious thought her hands moved to act as an automatic shield.

'Modesty, *agape*?' Loukas drawled with musing humour as he caught up the soap and began smoothing it along her arm.

'Why are you doing this?' Her voice sounded strangled, even to her own ears.

'Sharing your shower?' He turned her away from him and tended to her back, using long strokes that eased over her bottom and slid down to her knees…then crept up to encompass her shoulders. When he was done, he caught hold of her shoulders and turned her to face him.

'Don't.' It was a heartfelt plea he chose to ignore as he shifted her hands and palmed her breasts, lightly examined their soft fullness, then slid to the curve at her waist before slipping to the intimate vee between her thighs.

The brush of his fingers caused her body to arch, and she balled one hand into a fist and aimed for his chest.

Except he deftly fielded it before it could connect.

For a wild moment her eyes seared his own, and her lips formed a soundless gasp as he brought her fisted hand to his mouth and lightly brushed his lips across her knuckles.

His eyes were dark, heavy with lambent warmth, and she gave a startled cry as he clasped her shoulders and began to massage the taut muscles, easing in to loosen the kinks.

It felt so *good*, and she sighed as he rendered a similar treatment to her back, easing up to her neck to knead and soothe until she relaxed completely beneath his touch.

Not content, he massaged her head, and she closed her eyes and let her mind drift until he shifted her beneath the beating water to rinse the suds from her hair, her body.

Alesha turned to face him and swept her hands over her face to dispense the excess water.

'Better?'

'Much,' she admitted. 'Thank you.'

The stress of the day had diminished, together with the loosening of tense shoulder and neck muscles. Although there was a need to escape the confines of the shower stall…and the man who stood far too close for her peace of mind.

A wet naked man who with just a look could cause her body to go into sensual meltdown.

Did he know?

She hoped not. After Seth she'd vowed never to allow another man to get beneath her skin… *ever*.

Yet Loukas was steadily invading her senses, *there*…a strong magnetic force who managed to arouse feelings she hadn't known she possessed.

For one wild moment she wondered what it would be like to let go…to feel sufficiently secure to initiate sex and soar together in mutual delight. To gift him every sensual pleasure and *know* they were twin souls meant only for each other.

How emotionally freeing that must be.

Loukas glimpsed the faint wistfulness apparent, the fleeting emotions…and wondered if she knew how well he read her expressive features.

There was an urge to lift her high in his arms and take her, here, now. He could, easily. Except he wanted more than her mere compliance.

A quick coupling in the shower, invigorating as it would be for him, wouldn't be her idea of fun…yet. He was treading delicate ground, with the need to earn her trust…completely and without reservation. Something that required time, patience and care.

'I should go.' Did her voice sound as awkward as she felt?

His mouth formed a faint smile. 'You could stay and return the favour.'

Run the soap over his body? Reach for him?

'It's easy,' Loukas encouraged gently as he placed the soap in her hand and covered it with his own.

Her eyes flared as he brought the soap to his chest and began easing it in a slow circular pattern extending to his throat, the tops of his arms and down to his waist.

Easy? How could this kind of intimacy be *easy* when she'd never indulged in it before?

Especially when the man was Loukas…who steadily with every day and night that passed seemed to extend the boundaries in their marriage.

Worse, she found herself increasingly in a state of ambivalence…alternating longing for his tenderness, the promise of something more, yet nervously reluctant to accept it.

The nerves in her stomach tightened into a painful ball as memory provided vivid recall of Seth's unfeeling cruelty, both verbal and physical.

Don't…the word screamed silently inside her

head. Don't bring your ex into the equation.
There's no comparison between Seth and Loukas.

Focus on the now. You can do this.

Slowly, in gradual increments, the stroking of
soap combined with the hiss of hot water cascading
from the dual shower heads began to have a
soothing effect, and there was a sense of pleasure
verging on eroticism evident in washing a man's
body.

Not any man. Loukas, she admitted with a
degree of surprise.

Alesha avoided meeting his gaze as sensation
flared deep within and began to pulse through her
veins as fascination combined with reluctant admiration
for his superb musculature, defined and
sculpted by physical fitness. The slender waist,
the lean hips…dear God, the size of him in a state
of semi-arousal.

Surely he wouldn't take the soap there…except
he did, much to her embarrassment, although to
be fair he kept it clinical and he released his hand
from her own as he turned to present his back.

Not that it made much difference, and for a
brief few seconds she was strongly tempted to
throw down the soap and escape.

Instead, she began smoothing the soap across
the expanse of his shoulders, noting the flex of
powerful muscle tone as she swept long strokes

down to his waist and back to his shoulders until she'd covered every inch.

He possessed a tightly shaped butt...cute, she accorded, then she stilled in shock at the thought she might actually be deriving a degree of enjoyment in washing him.

When she was done he turned to face her, and colour flooded her cheeks as she saw he was fully aroused.

Ohmigod... *Chill*, she bade silently as she endeavoured to keep her breathing steady. It's just a normal male reaction.

Didn't *his* ministrations with the soap have a similar effect on you?

Had that been the object of the exercise?

She needed to get out of here *now*.

One wrong move...

'I'm sure you can manage the rest.'

With that, she stepped around him and pushed open the glass door, filched a folded towel from one of many stacked on a nearby rack and wrapped it round her slender form before collecting another to deal with her hair.

Alesha was dressed when he emerged, and she spared his impressive frame a quick glance. A white towel hitched at his hips accentuated his olive-toned skin, and her pulse quickened as he discarded it and pulled on briefs.

'I'll go check on dinner.'

They enjoyed a pleasant meal, sipped wine, and indulged in easy conversation. Loukas was a skilled raconteur, and she began to relax...until he mentioned the need to return to Athens for a short period of time.

'Business,' he relayed.

'How long will you be away?'

'We,' Loukas corrected, and saw her lips part in disbelief.

'You want me to go with you?'

'It's an opportunity to reconnect with the family.'

Alesha had met his parents and his younger sister several years ago when she'd accompanied her parents to Greece. Then she'd been a carefree young woman of twenty, in love with life, establishing her career with Karsouli and studying for an honours degree in business management.

A lot had happened in the intervening years. Now she was Loukas' wife, an equal partner in Karsouli, and all too aware Loukas' parents knew the facts surrounding their son's marriage.

How could she refuse...and on what grounds?

'We'll take an evening flight out tomorrow evening.'

So soon?

Athens. At this time of year the temperatures

would be similar, with autumn in one country and spring in another.

There was a part of her that looked forward to visiting the city again. The ancient and the new, the sense of history.

Playing the newly-wed wife beneath the keen eyes of Loukas' family was something else.

'I'll take these through to the kitchen and load the dishwasher.'

Loukas joined her, and set up the coffee-maker, then when it was ready he filled two cups, placed one on the servery and leaned a hip against its marble edge and spared her a dis-cerning look.

'We'll stay at my home in suburban Kifissia, then spend a few days on the island.'

Okay, she could do this. Like she had an option?

'Pack light. My mother and sister will undoubt-edly plan at least one shopping expedition.' He shifted to his full height and indicated his coffee. 'I'll take this with me and work for a few hours.'

A full day at the office and packing with lightning speed ensured Alesha didn't have time to *think*…which had to be a bonus.

Loukas, on the other hand, juggled everything with admirable expertise, filled a carry-on bag with essentials, and offered a musing smile as she queried, 'Is that all you're taking?'

'I have clothes in each of my homes.'

Of course. 'You lead a charmed life.' Not exactly fair, when he worked long hours between office and home, and achieved more in a day than most men accomplished in a week. What was more, he managed to do so with exemplary ease.

He crossed to her side, slid a hand to her nape and kissed her briefly, but with a thoroughness that left her catching her breath.

'Relax.'

Like she could do that when he invaded her senses and melted her bones?

He made her think of the impossible…only to dismiss it out of hand. They had a marriage. The beginnings of affection…maybe. It was enough. More than she'd expected. So why did she feel as if her emotions were spinning out of control?

Ridiculous, she chided silently as she tossed cosmetics and perfume into a bag and slotted it into a suitcase.

She caught up her shoulder bag. 'Shall we leave?'

A chartered Lear jet awaited them at Sydney airport, and, once airborne, Loukas opened his laptop and focused on work, while Alesha did likewise.

Although her father had preferred to travel via

a commercial flight, she admired the advantage of a chartered jet whose interior held luxurious recliner sleep chairs, together with designer office accessories enabling a corporate high-flier to work in comfort.

For the duration of the flight they both spent large slices of time on their laptops, ate, slept and took the occasional break.

Alesha found it stimulating to discuss Karsouli on a one-to-one basis; to present a few of her ideas for its future...proposals Dimitri had listened to, but not implemented due to lack of capital—something she hadn't known at the time.

The strategies Loukas intended—some of which were already in place—had her approval, and she could only applaud his long-term plan to return Karsouli to its former power amongst a global industry.

His keen mind, intelligence combined with a certain ruthlessness to elevate him sharing equal prestige with some of the world's known financial peers.

Qualities that offered a different perspective to the man who'd taken on the husband role...in a business arrangement that, for her, was becoming increasingly personal with every passing day.

Night, she corrected. For she couldn't deny she found comfort as he held her through the night.

To stir in sleep, and have him reach for her. The feel of his lips against the soft-beating pulse at the base of her throat. Just *knowing* he was there.

And the sex…more, so much more than she'd ever dreamed possible. Wondrous, exciting, magical.

But that's all it is, she reminded herself. Good sex is just…good sex, and not to be confused with a deeper emotion.

So…enjoy the ride and don't question the motives?

Fine, if you could separate the prosaic from the illusion.

After all, what was she to him other than a partner in every legal sense?

It was late afternoon when the Lear jet touched down in Athens, and they emerged to balmy sunshine, passed through Customs to be met by Loukas' driver, Cristos, who transported them via limousine to suburban Kifissia where luxury homes surrounded by trees and beautiful gardens exuded wealth.

Alesha's eyes widened slightly as the limousine turned into a gated entrance and eased to a halt outside the entrance to a double-storeyed palatial mansion.

'My home base,' Loukas informed her as he led

her into a large marble-tiled foyer where a middle-aged housekeeper, whom he introduced as Hera, greeted them. Cristos followed with their luggage.

'It's beautiful,' she complimented simply. Elegant, she added silently as he led her upstairs to their bedroom suite. Rich furnishings, solid furniture, imposing mirrors and artwork adorning the walls.

A very large home for one man, she perceived, although fitting given he headed the Andreou consortiums and doubtless entertained…business associates, as well intimate dinners *à deux* with women.

Had any of his former mistresses shared his home?

And what if they had? His past was his own.

He'd vowed fidelity…the question had to be whether he intended to abide by it.

Emotional introspection following a long international flight, comfortable though it had been, did not make for a good mix.

What she needed was a leisurely shower, a change of clothes, dinner and a good night's sleep…in that order.

The spacious bedroom suite held one bed, albeit king-size, two walk-in robes with adjoining dressing rooms, two en suites.

Alesha opened her bag, extracted fresh underwear, tailored trousers and a knit top, then she entered the en suite Loukas indicated as her own, ignored the temptation to linger overlong, and chose to sweep her hair into a careless knot atop her head, vetoed make-up with the exception of lip gloss and emerged some ten minutes later to discover Loukas in the process of pulling on a cotton shirt over chinos.

Heeled sandals lent her height and aided confidence, she added silently as she slid them on.

Hera had prepared a delicately flavoured moussaka, a greek salad, with fresh fruit to follow, and Alesha declined coffee in favour of tea, lingered over it and endeavoured to fend off an increasing weariness while experiencing envy of Loukas' apparent vitality.

How did he do that?

'Why don't you go up to bed? I have a few calls to make before I call it a night.'

It was all too easy to acquiesce, and she cast him a musing smile as she rose to her feet. 'Goodnight.'

'Sleep well.'

She did, almost as soon as her head touched the pillow, and she was unaware of Loukas' presence as he slid in beside her, or that he curved her in close against him.

* * *

Alesha murmured indistinctly as she slid into the dream, subconsciously aware the sound moved to a purr of pleasure as lips nuzzled the sensitive curve between her neck and her shoulder. Mmm, *nice*.

So, too, was the gentle drift of fingers over the delicate slope of her breast, and her mouth relaxed into a winsome smile as the tender peak hardened beneath their touch.

She shifted a little, unconsciously arching her body as the hand slid to her waist, explored the diamond pin at her navel, before tracing a pattern over her stomach.

A husky sigh emerged from her throat as a mouth fastened over one breast and gently suckled, sending sensation spearing through her body, and she groaned softly in the need to beg for more…only to give a satisfied moan of pleasure as deft fingers slid to the apex between her thighs and found her throbbing clitoris.

If this was a dream, she didn't want it to end, for the pleasure was so acutely intense it almost transcended into reality.

Afterwards she couldn't pinpoint precisely when she became aware of emerging consciousness…only that she did, and she reached for him.

'At last you wake, *agape mou*,' Loukas murmured with a husky chuckle.

'Uh-huh.' She captured his head and framed it

as she sought his mouth with her own in a piercingly sweet kiss that touched him more deeply than he thought possible.

It unleashed a primitive hunger he fought to control as he shaped her body and entered her in one unrestrained thrust, absorbing her startled cry as her vaginal muscles gripped his hardened length.

For several seemingly long seconds he remained still, gentling his mouth into an erotic supplication, then he began to move, slowly at first as he took her with him, her increasing urgency matching his own as they became consumed by electrifying passion.

Incandescent, primal…she cried out with the force of it, and held onto him, almost afraid to let go in case she shattered into a thousand pieces.

It was almost as if her whole body vibrated with the aftershock of sensation that was more than just sex.

Dear heaven, she couldn't even find the words to describe how she felt as she buried her mouth in the curve of his neck.

She was barely aware of the soothing brush of his hand along her spine, or the touch of his fingers working a tactile massage at her nape.

There was no sense of the passage of time… just the slowing of her ragged breathing as she became consumed by a sense of dreamy peace.

Too emotionally spent to do more than close her eyes and drift easily to sleep.

Loukas slid from the bed as the dawn lightened the sky, then showered; freshly shaven, he dressed in business attire and crossed to the bed and stood looking at his wife's softened features.

She slept curled to one side, a hand tucked beneath her cheek…rested, replete, her generous mouth slightly parted in the semblance of a smile.

He felt his body stir, and he banked down the urge to take her mouth with his own.

Except it wouldn't stop there, and regrettably there wasn't time. Cristos waited in the limousine to drive him into the city where he'd connect with Constantine, field a call from his mother, and attempt to vet the social activities Angelina had undoubtedly planned during his short visit.

Beginning with this evening's family dinner held in his parents' home.

Would Alesha recall he'd informed her of the invitation as she rested in his arms through the early morning hours?

Possibly not. Rather than wake her, he'd leave a message with Hera, call between meetings, and issue Cristos with instructions to accompany her wherever she wanted to go.

Alesha woke late, discovered she was alone, and gave a startled yelp as she checked the time.

Nine? Half the morning gone…and where was Loukas?

Then she remembered, and she shifted the bed-covers, took a shower, dressed in casual wear and made her way downstairs to the kitchen.

Hera relayed Loukas' message, then she made fresh coffee and offered croissants, fresh figs, Greek-style yoghurt, and currant bread with honey.

Alesha chose the figs and yoghurt, washed them down with coffee before taking a walk in the grounds.

The day was warm, the air stirred by a slight breeze, and she admired the meticulously kept garden borders framing beds filled with floral blooms.

Loukas' mansion nestled against a hillside and offered a stunning panoramic view of the city reaching to the port of Piraeus.

The place of her parents' birth, where they had grown up and married before choosing to relocate in Sydney.

There was a sense of timelessness, of an ancient age, often violent, as rulers fought for power and glory.

She moved away, and heard the insistent ring of

her cellphone as she paused to admire the swimming pool with its blue mosaic tiles, ornamental cupids at placed intervals spouting plumes of water.

The sound of Loukas' deep, slightly accented voice sent her pulse into a quickened beat.

'A quick call to say I'll be caught up all day and not in until around seven,' he enlightened her. 'We're due at my parents' home at eight.'

'I'll ensure I'm ready.' She waited a beat. 'Tough day?'

'Nothing I can't handle.' He paused to speak to someone. 'I'll see you tonight.'

An event Alesha prepared for with care, electing to wear classic black, killer heels, and subtle make-up with emphasis on her eyes. Hair—upswept or loose?

'Loose,' Loukas declared as he entered the bedroom and shrugged out of his suit jacket, then pulled his tie free.

'You think?'

He crossed to where she stood and framed her face, then kissed her. 'Shame you're already dressed. You could have shared my shower.'

'Not enough time.'

His eyes gleamed. 'I could always ring ahead and say we'll be delayed.'

'But you won't.' A wicked smile curved the

edges of her mouth. 'Besides, I prefer a lover with a slow hand.'

He trailed light fingers down her cheek. 'You'll keep.'

Constantine and Angelina resided in the southern suburb of Voula, in a luxurious home located at the top of Panorama.

Cristos deposited them at precisely eight, and no sooner did the limousine draw to a halt than the front door opened to reveal Loukas' parents, who moved quickly down the wide steps to offer an affectionate greeting before ushering them into a spacious foyer where a vision in black stood poised at the base of an elegant staircase.

Lexi, Loukas' young sister, all grown up in her early twenties, tall, dark-haired, impeccably dressed...the antithesis of the defiant teenager Alesha remembered from five years ago.

'Hi.' Lexi hugged him. 'You've given me the best gift of all...a sister.' She turned towards Alesha. 'Welcome.'

'Thank you.'

Lexi offered quietly, 'Thia Daria is waiting in the lounge to offer a formal greeting.'

Constantine's sister...a dour spinster, Alesha recalled, with an acerbic tongue, and wondered if perchance she'd mellowed a little since the last time they'd met.

Not a smidgen, if the woman's severe expression was any indication.

'So,' Daria began imperiously. 'You are the pawn Dimitri offered to save his wretched soul.'

Oh, my, this had all the portents of being a *fun* night.

'Hardly his soul.' She met the older woman's steely gaze and held it. 'He took that with him.'

'I speak the truth.'

'A truth I'm very aware of,' Alesha offered calmly. 'Did you imagine otherwise?'

'Loukas is my godson. As the only male Andreou of his generation, I consider it is of vital importance he has taken a wife worthy of bearing his name.'

'While I consider the importance lies with Loukas' ability to share equal partnership in Karsouli.'

Lexi clapped her hands lightly. 'Well fielded.'

Constantine indicated a collection of comfortable sofas. 'Please, be seated. I'll open the champagne.'

'I prefer ouzo.'

Naturally, Alesha conceded, Daria would take pleasure in being contrary. Was it a game? Maybe two could play…

Over dinner, perhaps.

A delicious meal prepared especially by

Angelina, comprising several courses...tasty samples of various seafood dishes, followed by mouth-watering sweet honey and nut pastries and fresh fruit.

It was during dessert that Daria made an announcement in the form of a statement...no one could possibly term it a suggestion, Alesha decided a trifle ruefully.

'You have denied your family the pleasure of participating in your wedding. A ceremony will be repeated here in Athens. Tomorrow,' she determined firmly, 'we will shop.'

'A reaffirmation of your marriage vows,' Angelina declared with enthusiasm. 'All that is required will be the documented proof the marriage has already taken place.' Her eyes sparkled. 'There will be guests...a party.' She paused for a few seconds. 'Afterwards you will take Alesha to the island for a few days,' she concluded.

Oh, my. The light touch of Loukas' hand on her thigh caused her to look at him askance.

'A charming idea.' His eyes speared her own. 'Alesha?'

That was right...throw the ball into her court! Like she was going to refuse? 'Charming,' she agreed. In a moment of inspiration she turned towards Lexi. 'I'd love it for you to be my attendant.'

'Done,' Loukas' sister concurred with delight.

'Which means I get to join in the shopping expedition.'

'It will be my pleasure. My gift to you both.' Constantine beamed as he sank back in his chair. 'And now we shall adjourn to the lounge and Angelina will bring the coffee.'

It was almost midnight when Loukas summoned Cristos and they took their leave.

Alesha settled into the rear seat of the limousine as Loukas joined her, and she sat in reflective silence as Cristos traversed the driveway.

Loukas reached for her hand and brought it to his lips. 'You managed very well.'

His features appeared as shadowed angles in the evening's darkness, illuminated by passing street-lighting and the beam of oncoming traffic.

'Your aunt is a lioness.'

'Yet beneath the surface lies the heart of a pussycat.'

'You're kidding me?'

'You're now part of the Andreou family. One Daria guards with her life. You will discover she is generous to a fault,' he relayed quietly. 'And very caring towards those who earn her trust.'

'You could have warned me what to expect.'

'Perhaps,' Loukas conceded. 'But would it have made any difference?'

No. For how could she have disappointed his

parents, Lexi…Daria, even, if she'd indicated a reaffirmation of her wedding vows was too much to ask?

'So we get to do it…when?'

'I imagine my mother and Daria already have the details in hand.'

Alesha didn't doubt it for a moment.

Sleep didn't come easily, and she sighed a little as Loukas drew her close and brushed his lips to her temple. 'You want me to help you sleep?'

'Depends what you have in mind,' she managed in a voice husky with tiredness.

'If I promise to do all the work?'

'Uh-huh.'

'I assume that's a *yes*?'

His light teasing held a sensuality that warmed her blood and sent it pulsing through her body. 'What are you waiting for?'

A faint chuckle emerged from his throat as he sought the softly beating pulse at the edge of her neck, savoured a little, then his lips trailed a path to her breast, suckled there, and moved low to create the sort of sensual havoc that demanded release…hers, by him.

He gifted it to her, eventually, and caught her as she climaxed. Then he held her for what remained of the night, sleeping as she slept until dawn crept over the horizon and gave birth to a new day.

CHAPTER NINE

LOUKAS' words 'have fun' echoed in Alesha's mind as Cristos drove to Voula, collected Angelina, Daria and Lexi, and headed towards one of several elite shopping areas in the city where designerwear graced exclusive boutiques.

Angelina and Daria quibbled and clicked their tongues as one gown after another was submitted for their approval…or not. Mostly it was not.

'Don't despair,' Lexi encouraged quietly. 'They both have excellent taste.'

And no regard whatsoever to cost, Alesha perceived, and gave up figuring the exchange conversion.

By comparison, it made shopping for *the* dress in Sydney with Lacey seem like a breeze.

'Lunch,' Daria announced. 'After which Cristos will take us on a tour of the city until the shops reopen.'

Although Alesha had explored some of the

tourist sights with her parents during her last visit to Athens, it proved interesting to revisit familiar places and hear a different perspective of the history. Tales passed by word of mouth through the generations, doubtlessly distorted by the passage of time, but there was a sense of admiration that some of the buildings had been painstakingly assembled without benefit of machinery so long ago.

To pass over ground trodden by an ancient civilization, where the blood of her ancestors had been spilt, and heretics were put to death.

Modern roads, homes, industry now covered ground that had once been barren. If one possessed an overly vivid imagination, it was almost possible to hear the thunder of galloping horses, the roar of men as they went into battle, the clash of swords.

A return to the city streets where some of the most famous shops were located ensured forays into a few, where recognition of the Andreou name resulted in almost obsequious attention.

'Today we look, we compare,' Angelina confided. 'Anything of particular interest we request a twenty-four-hour reserved hold. Tomorrow we return and decide.'

It was late when Cristos departed from the Andreou home in Voula and headed north to Kifissia.

All Alesha had to show for the day was one glossy designer-emblazoned bag.

She thanked Cristos when he deposited her outside the front door of Loukas' home, greeted Hera on entering the foyer, then she ran lightly upstairs to their suite, toed off her shoes, undressed and ran a bath where she luxuriated in a leisurely scented soaking before emerging to dry off and don a towelling robe.

Loukas entered the room as she caught the length of her hair and twisted it into a loose knot, which she fixed in place with a large clip.

'Hi, you're home,' she offered as he crossed the room to her side. The mere sight of him, his presence, invaded her senses, and her insides felt in serious danger of melting into an ignominious puddle as he framed her face and took her mouth with his own in a lingering kiss.

'You shared an enjoyable day?'

Alesha rolled her eyes. 'Do you have any idea how the female members of your family *shop*?'

'That bad, huh?'

'Don't you dare laugh,' she threatened.

'I wouldn't dream of it.' He rested light hands on her shoulders. 'Which ache the most…feet or shoulders?'

'Both,' she said succinctly, and almost groaned as his fingers sought out the kinks and knots and began to ease them with an expertise for which she could only thank him.

Heaven...he could have been a masseur in another life.

'Should I ask how many purchases have been made?'

'Shoes,' she offered. 'Even though I have a perfectly suitable pair of my own.' She lifted a hand, then let it fall to her side. 'Your mother has offered me her lace wedding veil.'

'I believe it's exquisite.'

'I thought this would be *simple*.'

'Shopping to my mother, Daria and Lexi is an art form,' Loukas assured her solemnly. 'And accorded due reverence.'

'Tomorrow we take up where we left off.' She turned slightly to look at him. 'There's no chance I can take a rain check and spend the day with you in the city office?'

'It would be more than my life is worth.'

'You're kidding me? The powerful omnipotent Loukas Andreou bows down to the three women in his life?'

'Four,' he corrected with an amused smile. 'You neglected to include yourself. And shopping, in this instance, is of the utmost importance.'

'I shall think of ways to make you pay,' she

threatened with dire emphasis, and heard his husky laugh.

'Sounds interesting.'

'Is this second wedding, for want of a better word, scheduled to happen *soon*?'

'Early next week, I believe.'

'You mean, you don't know for sure?'

'Tuesday has been mentioned.'

She could do this. The trick was to be more assertive and not allow the Andreou women to make *all* the decisions.

'Is there any social engagement I should be aware of?'

'A fundraiser on Saturday evening for a worthy charity Andreou has sponsored for a number of years.'

Consequently attendance would be expected together with the gift of a sizable donation. Which meant an Andreou bride would garner considerable interest.

But then, hadn't Loukas also drawn attention as her husband at a similar charitable event Karsouli supported in Sydney?

Wealthy tycoons were known to donate generously to worthy charitable causes. Most chose to give something back, with time and money for those genuinely in need. Committees organized events, provided entertainment and a three-course meal including alcoholic beverages…and charged accordingly.

It gave the social elite an opportunity to select designer gowns, wear their jewellery, be seen and the chosen few to appear in the media social pages.

'How was your day?' She hadn't thought to ask, and he removed his hands as she turned to face him.

'Busy. Constantine is considering semi-retirement. It means reshuffling a few executive staff, selecting suitable replacements and aligning a technical infrastructure I can oversee from Sydney.'

'And you're okay with his decision?' It would mean a heavier workload, possibly a reasonably regular commute between Sydney and Athens.

Would she accompany him? Somehow the thought of remaining in Sydney alone didn't hold much appeal. She'd miss his presence…sharing her bed, the pleasure of his touch through the night. Dammit…she'd feel as if a part of her were lost.

For a moment she couldn't think. Where had that come from? It meant she cared…when she'd silently sworn not to become emotionally involved.

A hollow laugh rose and died in her throat.

Sure, like that isn't the joke of the year!

'It's inevitable, given he's reached his early sixties.'

For a moment she looked at him blankly, for she'd lost the thread of their conversation.

She glimpsed the faint gleam in his dark eyes as he lifted a hand and traced light fingers down the vee of her robe, loosened the ties at her waist, then he shaped the slight weight of her breasts.

'Beautiful,' he complimented gently. He lowered his head and brushed his lips to each in turn, then he sought the faint scar beneath one sensitive peak, caressed it...and sensation speared through her body.

'You're wearing a new perfume.'

'It's soap,' she managed in a slightly strangled voice, and felt his mouth curve into a smile. 'Gardenia,' she added and gasped as he lifted his head and took possession of her mouth.

Magic, sheer magic, she registered dimly as she threaded her fingers through his hair and leant into the kiss, gifting as well as taking, absorbing everything he chose to give...and more.

It wasn't enough. She needed him, all of him, naked, skin on skin, his body fused with hers in a primitive mating, uniquely and exclusively *theirs* in a way there could never be another for either of them.

Was that *love*?

Lust, certainly. But surely love was a different entity, involving trust and fidelity.

And she couldn't love him...could she? Hadn't she sworn never to let another man get beneath her skin and steal her heart?

Yet Loukas was *there*, a constant in her thoughts, her mind. He managed to make her feel different, almost special. Was it merely a practised act in order to lull her into a false sense of security?

Sadly, she didn't know...and there was a part of her that didn't *want* to know. For to discover it was all a charade would hurt her more than she imagined possible.

And that, she recognized, was an admission in itself.

With effort, she eased back from him a little, aware he didn't attempt to dissuade her.

'You should go shower and change,' Alesha managed quietly. 'Or we'll be late for dinner.'

He touched a finger to her slightly swollen mouth. 'And that would never do, hmm?'

'I'm sure Hera has gone to considerable effort.'

Without a further word she crossed into her dressing-room, shed the robe, selected fresh underwear, and chose tailored trousers and a fashionable blouse...reappearing into the bedroom to find it empty and the sound of the shower running in Loukas' en suite.

Dinner was a pleasant meal, during which conversation didn't lag...although afterwards

Alesha retained little memory of what they'd actually discussed.

Loukas excused himself on the pretext of work, while she used her laptop to catch up with emails and respond to one of Lacey's that had landed in her inbox that morning.

It was late when she retired to bed, and even later when Loukas joined her. For a moment she lay perfectly still, unsure whether he'd reach for her or not…and when he curved her close in against him she wasn't sure whether to be relieved or peeved when his breathing slowed and acquired the steadiness denoting sleep.

The following few days were filled with shopping, and it came as a relief when the Andreou women conceded contented satisfaction in having achieved their objective.

Alesha had to admit they showed excellent taste in fashion, and she couldn't fault their suggested choices.

'Now you can relax,' Lexi confided as Cristos delivered them to Voula late Friday afternoon.

You *think*? Alesha posed silently.

With the charity fundraiser the following evening, the reaffirmation of marriage vows and party planned for Tuesday, *relaxing* wasn't a state she'd reach any time soon.

Daria, as Loukas had predicted, had mellowed considerably during the past few days, and it was possible to catch a glimpse of the woman beneath the severe exterior.

Angelina proved to be the quintessential mother, who had learnt to accept her son and daughter as adults in an adult world, and gained the wisdom to step aside from the strict parental role and respect them as equals. An admirable quality that Alesha found endearing.

Lexi's engaging personality made her easy to like, so too did her determination to strike out on her own.

'Loukas *is* Andreou. My talent lies with fashionable jewellery, specifically design. I have a studio in the Pláka, and a small degree of success. This year has brought exposure, and I will soon need to take on another staff member.'

'So when do I get to see some of your designs?' Alesha asked as they shared coffee in the lounge after a dinner Angelina had insisted she share when Loukas had called to say he would be dining with associates and not due home until late.

'I'll give you the link to my website, and we'll fit in a time for Cristos to bring you to the studio before you return with Loukas to Sydney. Sound good?'

'I'll look forward to it.'

It was almost eleven when Cristos delivered

her home, and her cellphone beeped as she headed upstairs.

'Another hour, *agape mou*,' Loukas relayed in his slightly accented drawl.

'I'll probably be asleep.'

'In which case I'll wake you.'

The mere thought of being woken by him sent delight slithering down the length of her spine. 'If you must.'

His soft chuckle almost undid her.

Alesha undressed and headed into the shower, set the water dial to hot and let the heat soothe away the stress of the day as she lathered her body with the gardenia-scented soap…and attempted to convince herself the choice had nothing to do with Loukas.

Caught up in reflective introspection, she attempted to analyze when her emotions had begun to change from reluctantly accepting the marriage…to wanting it to work, to be real.

To love, and be loved in return? Was that too much to ask for?

Yet love couldn't be bought. It was built on emotion, and deserved the utmost care.

In a moment of self-indulgence she let her mind wander to the years ahead…children Loukas would lift high in the air and laugh with in their tender years, be fiercely protective of as they grew, and encourage to achieve in all areas of their lives.

Wishful thinking didn't mean it would happen, and with fresh resolve she closed the water, caught up a towel and dried off before donning sleep pants and a singlet top.

On the verge of sleep she heard the faint click as Loukas closed the bedroom door, the soft rustle of clothing being discarded, followed by the sound of the shower.

Long minutes later he slid beneath the covers and reached for her, turning her easily in his arms as she caught his head and brought his mouth down to her own in a hungry kiss that stirred his senses to fever pitch.

This…*this* was what he'd consciously anticipated as he'd wined and dined three associates while negotiating a deal. One that had taken skilled strategy and patience to achieve.

Now he wanted to bury himself in the sweet sorcery of a woman's body. Not any woman… *this* woman.

To pleasure her until he sensed the soft purr in her throat as she arched her body against his own. The faint moan of capitulation as he nuzzled the sensitive hollow at the curve of her neck. Her reaction to his touch, the intimacy they shared… and the joy of mutual orgasm.

On the edge of sleep he gathered her close, soothed her when she stirred and held her through the night.

Alesha dressed with care, aware the silk chiffon gown with its ruched bodice in deep sapphire hugged her slender curves and highlighted the texture of her skin. The diagonally cut skirt flowed gently to rest at her ankles, and her heeled pumps and evening clutch were a perfect match.

Jewellery was restricted to a diamond pendant, ear-studs and matching bracelet.

She ensured her make-up was understated with emphasis on her eyes, a touch of bronzing powder and a soft neutral lipstick and gloss.

'Beautiful,' Loukas complimented as she prepared to precede him from the room, and she threw him a faintly teasing look.

'Thanks.'

Her eyes sparkled as she subjected him to a sweeping appraisal.

Attired in a black evening suit, fine white linen shirt and black bow tie, he looked far too compelling for any woman's peace of mind…especially hers.

'I guess you'll do.'

His soft laughter curled round her heartstrings and tugged a little. 'Damned with faint praise.'

Together they descended the staircase and moved to the front entrance where Cristos waited with the limousine.

'Anything more and you'll get a swelled head,' she said solemnly as she slid into the rear passenger seat. Her pulse leapt as he captured her hand and held it for the duration of the drive into the city.

The hotel hosting the event had to be one of the city's finest, Alesha perceived as she stood at Loukas' side amongst the mingling guests sipping champagne.

Men of varying ages wore formal evening wear while the women sparkled…literally, in jewellery worth a fortune.

She became aware her presence garnered speculative interest, and she tilted her head a little, kept a smile in place, and maintained an expected pretence.

It was something of a relief when Constantine, Angelina, Daria and Lexi joined them.

'The rescue team,' Lexi enlightened her quietly as she leant forward to brush her lips to Alesha's cheek. 'You look gorgeous.'

'Same goes.' A genuine compliment as Loukas' sister wore a stunning gown in fire-engine red that showcased her figure with breathtaking style.

Daria looked regal in black, while Angelina had opted for delicate shades of lilac.

'Would you like a rundown on some of the guests?' Lexi queried lightly. 'Or would you prefer to form your own impression?'

'You think it'll make a difference?'

'Not in the slightest,' Lexi assured her. 'Although I shall warn you of any impending danger.'

She couldn't help a faint laugh. 'Loukas' ex-girlfriends?'

'Plural? You're quick. One in particular.'

'Do I get a name?'

'Iliana,' Lexi informed her with droll humour. 'Model, filthy rich, and hunting Loukas. Expect a cat-fight when she discovers he's taken.'

'As she will?'

'Darling Alesha. News travels fast.'

So it did, in any city in the world. Why should Athens be any different?

'Approaching from the right,' Lexi voiced softly several minutes later. 'Wearing black and white.'

Stunning, tall, incredibly slender, with exquisitely assembled facial features, luminous dark eyes and a mouth that promised much.

Oh, my. Perfection personified, Alesha conceded as Iliana drew close.

'Kalispera.'

The greeting included each of them, but the model's attention rested solely on Loukas.

'Iliana.' His voice held a coolness that was ignored.

'You have a relative join you tonight?' The assumption held a teasing lightness that wasn't reflected in her eyes, and Alesha was willing to swear all three Andreou women drew in their collective breaths.

'My wife, Alesha,' Loukas relayed in a silky drawl, and merely compounded the situation by taking hold of Alesha's hand and raising it to his lips.

'How…adventurous of you, darling,' Iliana arched, 'when a legal commitment was never on your agenda.' She paused to summon a slight, deliberately fake smile. 'Although there is the duty to produce an Andreou heir.'

The woman was all feline with vicious claws, Alesha perceived, and doubtless ate unsuspecting men for breakfast.

It posed the question as to how deeply involved she'd been with Loukas.

Even the thought of the model's sinuous body wrapping itself around him made Alesha feel slightly nauseous.

She gave herself a mental shake. *Get real.* He's no celibate. It's a given there have been women… probably scads of them. So what?

But *Iliana*?

How could she hope to compete?

'Do you not speak?' the model posed with the glitter of revenge momentarily apparent in her dark eyes.

'When I have something to say.'

She sensed Lexi's faint smile, and mentally braced herself for Iliana's next verbal parry.

'It doesn't bother you that Loukas and I are intimate friends?'

'Should it?'

'Enough.' One word, quietly delivered, but only a fool would ignore the steel beneath Loukas' silky voice.

Daria offered a comment in her own language… words Alesha had no difficulty in comprehending.

The evening didn't improve as Iliana boldly took her place at their table, ignored Daria and Angelina's telling looks as she proceeded to stake a claim for Loukas' attention.

To his credit he mostly ignored her, adhering only to polite civility as the occasion demanded.

Yet it made for unnecessary awkwardness, and doubtless aroused speculation amongst many of the guests present.

Alesha recalled the words of a famed socialite who advised… *'Don't get mad, darling—get even.'*

So she smiled, conducted animated conversation with their table companions, and managed to cast Loukas an adoring look or three during the meal.

It helped that he played a similar part, although there was a bad moment when Alesha and Lexi used the powder room, and Iliana entered as they were about to exit.

Alesha witnessed the gleam of satisfaction in the model's eyes, and mentally prayed a verbal war could be avoided.

'Very clever of you, darling, to land a fish of Loukas' calibre. What bait did you use?'

'Public displays are a trifle tacky,' she ventured as Iliana initiated a confrontation. 'Don't you think?'

'Are you pregnant?'

'Iliana,' Lexi said quietly. 'You're in danger of making a fool of yourself.'

Alesha placed a placating hand on Lexi's arm and held the model's gaze as she asked evenly, 'Is there a point to this conversation?'

Hard eyes raked a damning appraisal. 'You're quite pretty. But don't think your marriage will last. Loukas is an intensely sexual animal. I doubt you'll satisfy him for long.'

'You think? Perhaps I should thank you for the advice and suggest more creative positions...'

she paused deliberately '…in places other than the bedroom.'

The colour leeched from Iliana's face, then flooded back as her hand flew towards Alesha's face.

A move Alesha stalled with galling ease. 'Don't,' she warned quietly.

'Or you'll do…what?'

'This.' She sought the right nerve and the model's legs buckled, sending her sliding to the floor.

With incredible calm she turned towards Lexi. 'Shall we leave?'

'My God,' Lexi breathed in stunned surprise as they gained the ballroom and headed towards their table. 'Where did you learn to do that?'

She bore Lexi's speculative look. 'It's a long story.'

'That's what I thought.'

Loukas' gaze seared her own as she slid into her seat.

'Problems?'

'Interesting question. Would that be singular or plural?'

'Iliana.'

'Astute of you.'

Lexi leaned forward. 'Alesha was magnificent.'

His eyes didn't leave her own. 'Indeed?'

'You had to be there,' his sister relayed.

'That particular Jezebel needs to be taken down a peg,' Daria opined sternly, whereupon her niece grinned unashamedly.

'*Thia*, Alesha did…literally.'

'Good.'

A backhanded compliment from Loukas' dour aunt? Accompanied by an approving smile? *Incredible*.

It was interesting to note the seat Iliana had occupied at their table remained empty. Had the model left the event? Somehow Alesha didn't think so.

A fact that was confirmed half an hour later as the focus of the evening featured a fashion parade by three of Athens' top designers with models showing a selection ranging from casual chic to evening wear.

It came as no surprise Iliana formed part of the group of models hired for the evening.

Alesha had to concede the model's professionalism, for her figure bore the perfect lines to showcase the garments to maximum effect.

The personal touches, however, were a deliberate payback as Iliana tossed her long mane of gloriously wavy hair and pouted a little too prettily as she gazed overlong at Loukas.

An effort to show him what he was missing?

Maintaining an interested expression took some effort, and Alesha shot Loukas a startled look as he took hold of her hand and soothed the rapidly beating pulse at the base of her wrist.

This was meant to be reassurance? *Please.*

She endeavoured to tell herself it didn't matter…but it did.

To a degree she felt exposed, even vulnerable, knowing there had to be a number of guests present who were aware Loukas and Iliana were once an item. Given how gossip travelled, it was now common knowledge Loukas had taken a wife. Cue in Iliana's public display on the catwalk, and it wasn't difficult to do the maths.

She'd ridden out worse with the fallout from her experience with Seth. What was a model's wrath in comparison?

So she continued to smile and converse, and generally project the image of someone enjoying the event. Her demeanour earned a surprisingly gentle smile from Daria, as if she knew and saw all…which she probably did.

The charity chairperson thanked the assembled guests for their generosity, and gave a closing speech.

Filtered music provided a muted background and there was a general shift as businessmen converged, while women took the opportunity to catch up with friends seated elsewhere.

An elderly man sought Loukas and Constantine's attention, and both men excused themselves from the table to converge into a group of three a short distance away.

'I'll be at my studio on Monday, if you'd like to call in,' Lexi offered, and Alesha responded with enthusiasm.

'Love to. Give me a time and I'll be there.'

'Eleven? Then we can do lunch.'

'Done.'

Loukas returned to her side, and when she attempted to extricate her hand from his, he made the exercise more difficult by threading her fingers through his own.

Eventually the evening came to a close and the guests rose to leave...a lengthy process as the ballroom slowly emptied and guests spilled into the foyer to mingle as the concierge directed cars be brought to the entrance.

'Tuesday will be splendid,' Daria declared as she bestowed a light kiss to Alesha's cheek. 'Have faith, my dear.'

This was the same Daria, she of the acerbic tongue? Perhaps it was a rite of passage, from which she'd emerged having gained Daria's approval.

Constantine's driver appeared with their limousine, followed immediately by Cristos, ensuring farewells were exchanged and both limousines moved quickly away from the hotel entrance.

CHAPTER TEN

LOUKAS turned towards her as the large car eased into traffic. 'Now would be a good time to tell me what went down with Iliana.'

Alesha didn't pretend to misunderstand. 'The powder-room incident?'

'That's the one.'

'You could ask Lexi.'

'I'm asking you.'

'Do you need me to draw a verbal picture?'

'Iliana is a diva, with the temper to match.'

'Like I didn't get the drift of both?' Or her obsession with *you*? she added silently. 'Okay, words were said, and Iliana took umbrage.'

'That's it?'

'Not exactly.'

'There's more?'

'I—used preventive measures to avoid being slapped.'

There was a few seconds' pause, and his voice

assumed a musing drawl. 'And how, precisely, did you manage that?'

She looked at him carefully and could detect little from his expression in the dim light. 'Precisely?'

'Please.'

'Nerve pressure.'

'I'm almost afraid to ask.'

Alesha told him.

He lifted her hand and brushed his lips across her knuckles. 'You want me to say there were few women before you?'

'Not according to the media.'

'Would it help if I assured you that I ended a relationship before beginning another, and practised fidelity with each lover?'

'You want marks for integrity?'

It was late when they bade Cristos goodnight and entered the house. Loukas reset the security alarm and followed her upstairs to their bedroom.

The catch fastening on her pendant proved elusive again, and she gave a frustrated sigh as she tussled with it.

Then he was there, freeing the catch with ease, and she felt his fingers move to the zip fastener on her gown, felt the faint slide, followed by the slither of fabric as it slipped to the floor.

She turned to face him and eased off his jacket, then undid his tie and reached for the shirt buttons, freeing each one with deliberate slowness before releasing the fasteners holding his trousers in place.

He dispensed with his shoes, socks, and stepped out of his trousers.

'I want you naked.'

When he complied, she led him to the bed, then pushed him down onto the mattress.

'Stay.'

He lifted his arms, cupped his head and met her determined gaze with quizzical amusement. 'You want to play?'

Alesha merely smiled as she placed one knee on the mattress and straddled him. In one glorious movement she arched her body, then she lowered her head to brush the length of her hair across his chest, trailing it down until it rested on his arousal, tracing the sensitive skin back and forth as she heard his breath hiss through his teeth.

A satisfactory murmur of appreciation escaped her lips as she tossed her hair back before shaping him with gentle fingers…light, teasing strokes that caused his stomach muscles to tauten, then clench as she replaced her fingers with her mouth and stroked him with her tongue, bestowing feathery kisses until he hauled her close and took her mouth with his own.

'Uh-huh,' she cautioned. 'I'm not done yet.'

It became a leisurely exploration as she stirred his senses to fever pitch, teasing with gentle nips of her teeth, only to soothe with the tip of her tongue.

His male nipples earned her fascination, and he groaned as she circled him with her mouth, taunted with the edge of her teeth…then it was she who cried out as he clasped her hips and surged into her. Again and again, with a ravaging hunger that blew her away, and then some.

Cataclysmic sex. Passion at its most wild and wanton.

Primal.

Gradually their breathing slowed, and he pulled her down and held her close to nuzzle the sensitive curve at the base of her neck.

Her body trembled as he trailed a hand down the length of her spine and gently pressed its base, heard her soft sigh, then he slid a hand beneath her nape and kissed her so gently it made her want to cry.

She didn't want to move…didn't think she was capable as he feathered light fingers over the curve at her waist, shaped her buttocks, and simply held her.

There were no words for what they'd just shared, and she didn't even try to voice them.

At some stage she must have drifted into a dreamless sleep, for she came awake slowly to the sound of gushing water and an awareness she was alone in the bed.

The scent of gardenia teased her nostrils and she lifted her head as Loukas appeared from the en suite and scooped her into his arms.

There was no sense of time as he stepped into the bath and lowered her down to sit in front of him. With care he applied the soap to her skin as she caught her hair and pinned it high so it wouldn't get wet.

Her eyes searched his, and her heart melted beneath the warmth of his smile.

He was a gorgeous man, and he was hers.

There were words she wanted to say, but they remained locked in her throat.

He'd taught her to trust again, helped to restore her faith in men...one man, she corrected silently. The pieces of her heart were fusing together, almost making that life-force whole and complete so that it beat for him.

Only him.

To be with him like this was heaven. Everything she could ask for...

The soporific effect of warm scented water combined with his ministrations lulled her almost to the edge of sleep, and she smiled as he lifted her out, then enveloped her in a large bath towel, dried her, then he blotted the excess water from his body, released the bath plug...and carried her back to bed.

He gathered her close, touched his lips to her temple, and felt her mouth part with pleasure as she snuggled in against him.

Lexi's studio was situated in a trendy part of the city, where small shops competed with cafés and bars, boho chic wear, hand-tooled leather goods and stores selling organic foods. 'I'll call when I'm done,' Alesha assured Cristos as she alighted from the limousine and crossed the street to where Lexi stood waiting.

'Hi,' she greeted and shared a quick hug. 'I'm really looking forward to today.'

Lexi indicated a set of stairs. 'Let's go on up.' She led the way, and Alesha followed. 'The studio is only small. Cosy,' she elaborated over her shoulder.

But so interesting, Alesha accorded as she saw the various shaped casting moulds, metals, tools of trade, and a glass case with finished pieces on display.

A young girl and a guy in his mid-twenties worked with intricate pieces of metal, using specialized tools with an expertise she could only admire.

Enamelled flower brooches and pins, exquisite pendants, ear-studs, bracelets, dress rings, each individually designed and crafted.

'You have tremendous talent,' she compli-mented with sincere admiration. An enamelled bracelet set in gold caught her attention... It was utterly beautiful, the teal and blue melded per-fectly.

It was fascinating to learn the varying stages between design and completion, marketing and distribution.

There was little awareness of the passage of time, until Lexi glanced at her watch and declared they'd break for lunch.

'A delightful café not far from here does won-derful food. Their baklava is to die for.'

'Sounds good.'

It was everything Lexi said, authentic, family owned and well patronized.

'You'll adore the island,' Lexi relayed as they sipped coffee. 'It's a private sanctuary reached only by boat and helicopter.'

'Hey, Lexi.'

Alesha glanced towards two young men who pulled up two chairs to share their table. Mid to late twenties, she estimated, attired in jeans and tee shirts, and attractive.

Lexi introduced them as friends from her uni-versity days who ran a graphic art studio not far from her own.

They ordered coffee and food, and proved to be

good company as they chatted, laughed, and exchanged anecdotes.

'So you are the lady who managed to snare Loukas with a love net,' came the teasing observation.

The jury was still out on that one. Affection, great sex...but she doubted she had his heart.

'Mention his name, and the man himself appears.'

Lexi raised a hand in greeting as Loukas moved towards their table. 'I told Loukas we would be lunching here. He said he might join us.'

Alesha felt her pulse kick into a faster beat as he drew close, and her eyes widened a little when he lowered his head and brushed his lips to her cheek.

She met his dark gleaming gaze and offered a warm smile as he pulled up a chair, ordered, then curved an arm over the back of her chair.

Staking a claim?

Perhaps, Loukas mused, tussling a little with his reaction to seeing his wife enjoying the company of Lexi's two male friends.

He didn't like another man sitting close to his woman—*his* by marriage, by circumstance. But it was more than that. Affection, the need to protect.

Desire—*his*—for her. She'd crept beneath his

skin, invaded his senses…dammit, with each passing day she came closer to capturing his heart.

Something no other woman had achieved.

Last night…*Theos*…even thinking about her deliberately tactile teasing with her hands, her mouth…and it took all his control to rein in his arousal.

It made him want to take hold of her hand and lead her to the nearest room, somewhere private, preferably with a bed.

He couldn't remember being so in need of a woman. Alesha, only *Alesha*, for no one else came close.

His body clenched tight and he barely masked the glitter of expectation and anticipation, threatening to reveal his desire to anyone who happened to look closely enough.

Did she know?

Possibly not. She had yet to reach the place where she could read him. Or could it be she subconsciously resisted allowing herself to do so?

Slowly, surely, he was earning her trust. She felt comfortable with him…except he wanted more than that. He wanted it all. Everything.

To see her face light up when he entered the room. For her to come to him and gift herself with joy and no reservation.

He'd rescheduled an appointment…something he almost never did, except in extenuating circumstances, and had been quietly surprised at the ease with which he'd done so.

To join his wife for lunch, for heaven's sake. He, who always put business matters before anything or anyone else.

An hour later he rose to his feet, paid the bill, then contented himself with framing his wife's face as he kissed her thoroughly…and derived a certain satisfaction in seeing her cheeks colour a soft pink when he released her.

Minutes later Loukas walked from the café and had Cristos drive him to the city block where Andreou owned a building.

Whereupon Lexi's two friends indicated a need to return to their studio, and Lexi regretfully said she should do the same.

Alesha opted to browse some of the shops lining the Pláka before calling Cristos to collect and drive her to Kifissia.

Dinner was a leisurely meal, after which Alesha checked emails and touched base with her Sydney PA, while Loukas secluded himself in his home office.

Constantine and Angelina generously opened their magnificent home to host the renewal of vows ceremony presided over by an official and attended by family and numerous guests.

It was held late afternoon on a luxury terrace setting overlooking beautiful gardens. Alesha walked with Constantine behind Lexi along a rich carpet strewn with rose petals towards an arbour where Loukas stood waiting for her.

The ankle-length gown of cream slipper satin skimmed her slender curves, and Angelina's lace veil added the perfect touch.

The ceremony seemed almost surreal, conducted in Greek, and concluded with a special blessing as Loukas slid a stunning diamond solitaire ring onto her finger.

Alesha lifted her face as he drew her close and bestowed a gentle kiss to the accompanying sound of clapping from the assembled guests.

It was incredibly special, and so different from the civil ceremony in Sydney weeks ago when she'd felt filled with doubt and resentment.

Now there was a sense of hope their future together would bring happiness and contentment. Possibly *love*…although maybe that was expecting too much.

It was easy to accept congratulations from the guests, to smile and sip champagne, and enjoy the splendid dinner Angelina and Daria had organized exclusive caterers to serve.

Coloured lanterns provided illumination as dusk became night, and there was music and dancing, conviviality and laughter.

Loukas rarely moved from her side, and she became supremely conscious of the light touch of his hand at the edge of her waist…the gentle brush of his fingers as they traced the length of her spine.

He made her feel special, as if he cared. And she began to long for that elusive something that seemed just beyond her reach.

There were words she wanted to say, except she felt tentative in voicing them in case he failed to reciprocate in kind. How humiliating would that be?

Perhaps actions were enough. The way she kissed him, made love with him…*to* him. Wasn't that a language in itself?

If so, how could he not know?

Yet there was a part of her that wanted the words…his, wherein she'd *know* she held his heart as she'd gifted him her own.

To release every last vestige of doubt so joy could invade every cell in her body, every throbbing pulse-point…and fill her heart.

Maybe while they holidayed on the island, alone except for a housekeeper and caretaker. Warm sunshine to bask beneath, crystal-clear waters in which to swim, and soft balmy nights.

Just the two of them.

The guests stayed late and partied, and when the hour reached midnight Loukas caught hold of her hand, family and guests formed a loose circle, and together they personally thanked and bade every guest goodnight.

Cristos, whom Loukas had insisted join the guests, brought the limousine out front as everyone assembled outside the main entrance to provide a cheering send-off as Loukas handed Alesha into the rear seat before moving round the rear of the car to join her.

The drive to Kifissia held a certain magic as Loukas took hold of her hand and linked his fingers through her own.

It had been a beautiful day…a glorious evening, and she said as much.

'Thank you.' She turned to search his features and saw his smile.

'For what, specifically?'

'Agreeing to indulge your parents and Daria to arrange a second wedding on Greek soil.'

'It meant a lot to them to do so.'

'I know.' And she did know. To bring happiness into the lives of loved ones was a special gift.

'My ring is beautiful,' Alesha offered as she touched the exquisite solitaire resting above her wedding band. 'I didn't think about a gift. I have nothing for you in return.'

'Yes, you do. *You.*'

Did hearts melt? She was sure hers did. Together with every bone in her body.

'That's a...' she paused to gather the right words together, and faltered '...lovely compliment.' If only you mean it, she added silently.

For the first time she felt as if she knew where *home* was.

Not bricks and mortar in any country in the world. For it mattered little whether it was Sydney, Athens or other cities elsewhere.

It was Loukas. Knowing she'd follow him wherever he chose to lead. For without him she was nothing.

Love?

Wouldn't that be the ultimate irony?

She, who had wanted a paper marriage with no emotional involvement. Who had fought so hard to gain emotional independence after a disastrous first marriage...and who had vowed never to love again.

Alesha became aware the limousine had drawn to a halt, and she cast a surprised glance at the front entrance of Loukas' Kifissia mansion. She'd been so lost in contemplative reflection she hadn't noticed the passage of time.

Minutes later she entered the foyer and gasped

as Loukas placed an arm beneath her thighs and swept her into his arms.

'What is this?' she demanded in laughing query.

'I believe it's referred to as carrying one's new wife over the threshold,' he drawled with amusement as she wrapped her arms around his neck.

'And?'

He began ascending the stairs. 'An indication the night is far from over.'

'Really?'

Loukas touched his lips to her temple. 'Indeed.'

'Sounds promising.'

They reached the landing and he took the wide hallway leading to their bedroom.

'It's my intention to drive you wild.'

Sensation spiralled through her body, and she brushed her fingers over his beautiful mouth. 'Oh.'

He entered the bedroom and kicked the door shut, then released her in a slow slide down his body to stand on the floor.

'Just...*oh, agape*?' he teased as he carefully removed the veil from her hair.

'I'm lost for words.' She urged his suit jacket over his shoulders and tossed it onto a nearby chair as he reached for the zip fastening of her gown.

'I doubt *words* will form part of your vocabulary.'

She dealt with the buttons on his shirt, pulled it free and reached for the waistband of his trousers.

'Payback for last night?'

Her gown slithered to the floor, and she stepped from the puddle of slipper satin.

He buried his mouth into the soft scented hollow at the base of her throat. 'I promise to deliver.'

He did.

With such consummate skill, she didn't have any breath left in her body to do more than subside against him, totally spent…aware he'd brought every sensory cell achingly alive with a pleasure so intense it had been almost more than she could bear.

It was mid-morning when Cristos deposited them outside the main entrance to the Andreou building where a helicopter waited on the helipad at roof level to transport them to the island.

Within minutes of their boarding and being secured in their seats the rotors kicked in to a higher speed, then the helicopter lifted effortlessly into the air and began its flight over city buildings to the deep blue sparkling waters of the Aegean sea.

The scenery was magic as several islands, both

large and small came into view. Some bore small towns, hillside homes, hosting a populated community and geared to the tourist trade. While others bore small villages and olive groves. Then there were those tiny uninhabited islands covered in overgrown shrubbery.

Loukas pointed out a few privately owned islands and relayed their fascinating history, then he indicated another that had been owned by one of Greece's famed shipping magnates and used as a holiday home where his moored luxury cruiser hosted parties for the rich and famous.

The Andreou-owned island was small, with only thirty-odd acres of land, five of which had been levelled to hold a beautiful double-storeyed home whose stark white-painted stucco and brilliant blue-tiled roof epitomized Greek island architecture.

As the helicopter began to lose height Alesha saw luscious green lawn surrounding the house, garden borders, the dappled waters of a swimming pool and a tennis court. There was a designated helipad, and a separate cottage where, Loukas explained, the manager and his wife resided.

A middle-aged couple came forward as the helicopter rotors slowed, and Loukas introduced Spiros and Sofia, who offered an affectionate greeting before Spiros moved to take their bags from the helicopter.

'Magical,' Alesha accorded as she viewed the grounds. An idyllic haven, she added silently, far away from the hectic pace of a bustling city, and absent from any tourist trade.

The interior of the house bore tiled floors with patterned rugs of varying sizes, ivory-painted walls, solid furniture and modern amenities powered by a generator.

A comfortable home designed to promote relaxation with its spacious covered terraces and airy rooms.

The perfect private sanctuary, Alesha commended as she viewed the large bedroom offering splendid views over a small cove and beyond.

'I have prepared lunch,' Sofia informed. 'An evening meal is in the refrigerator to be heated in the microwave when you are ready to eat.'

'Thank you,' Alesha said with polite sincerity, and Sofia's smile widened.

'It is a pleasure.'

Minutes later she heard the faint click as the front door closed, followed by Sofia's footsteps as she trod the path to her cottage.

'Come here,' Loukas beckoned quietly, and she cast him a faintly wicked grin.

'You can't possibly be considering sex before lunch.'

'No?'

He was deliberately teasing her, and she poked a cheeky tongue in his direction. 'I have plans.'

One eyebrow slanted and his dark eyes gleamed with amusement. 'You do?'

'Uh-huh.'

'Do I get to hear about them, or do you intend to surprise me?'

'We play during the day. Swim, play tennis, sunbathe, maybe take that small boat out I saw moored to the jetty and catch fish.'

'You want to catch fish?'

'It's therapeutic,' she managed solemnly, and heard his quiet laughter.

'And the night?'

'Oh, I don't think you'll have anything to complain about there.'

'And now?'

'We explore, maybe swim before lunch.'

'Tennis in the afternoon?' he posed, and she inclined her head.

'It's called "keeping active",' she managed with a straight face.

'I can think of an infinitely more pleasurable activity.'

'Imagine the anticipation,' she offered with a wicked smile. 'And focus on the mutual reward.'

She was something else.

She'd been a tense young woman who held a fear

of intimacy, and he'd taught her to trust again and gradually the barriers she'd erected in self-protection had diminished until they no longer existed.

'You're proposing we change into casual clothes, pull on trainers and explore?'

Her eyes lost their teasing gleam and became serious.

'Do you mind?'

He caught hold of her hand and drew her into the circle of his arms. 'For you…anything,' he said quietly as he lowered his head and kissed her.

So very thoroughly she gave serious thought to discarding any plan that took them away from this room.

'That *almost* worked,' she offered with a tremulous smile when Loukas lifted his head.

'I could always put more effort into it.'

'Do that, and we'll never get out of here.'

The corners of his mouth lifted as he released her.

'Explore, I think you said?'

It became a light fun-filled day, followed by a night of slow loving that took them to a place where passion flared and ignited every sensory cell in her body. Followed by an aftermath of such piercing sweetness she prayed it would never end.

On the edge of sleep she had to wonder if it was the same for him.

Each day brought them even closer together, and Alesha adored the light teasing quality they exhibited with each other. The shared laughter as they swam laps in the pool, walked along the sandy foreshore, and played tennis.

There was the occasional hour spent in the electronically equipped office, as they checked emailed reports from Athens and Sydney and despatched emails in response.

Lacey wrote every few days relaying amusing anecdotes on life and love from her own perspective…and queried when Alesha and Loukas intended returning to Sydney.

All too soon the island idyll would end, Alesha recognized with regret. Yet the real world awaited, and perhaps in another year they'd return to enjoy another relaxing sojourn.

It was early Friday morning when a call came through from Constantine citing a problem requiring Loukas' urgent attention. One involving an emergency meeting in the Athens' office. The helicopter was on its way to collect him.

'I have—'

'To be there,' Alesha said at once. 'I know.'

In a short space of time a business suit replaced casual gear, and she accompanied him outside as the sound of the helicopter rotors drew close.

'I'll call you.' Loukas covered her mouth briefly

with his own, then he climbed into the cabin, belted the harness and attached a headset as the pilot increased the rotor speed…then they were in the air.

Alesha re-entered the house, poured herself a second cup of coffee and contemplated the day ahead without him. So she'd go for a walk along the beach, then persuade Sofia to reveal recipes for some of the delicious meals she'd served them. She could spend time on her laptop, slot in a DVD…and wait for Loukas to call.

Which he did as she ate lunch.

'There's a complication,' he relayed. 'I'm about to head into another meeting. I could be late.'

Resolve it and hurry back, I miss you… Words she refrained from voicing. 'Take care.'

'I'll call as I board the helicopter.' Then he cut the connection.

CHAPTER ELEVEN

THE phone rang late afternoon, and Alesha picked up on the third peal.

'Loukas?'

'Alesha?' Not Loukas' voice, but that of a woman, and she answered cautiously.

'Yes?'

'Eleni Petrakis, Loukas' PA.'

Her heart sank a little. Something had come up and Loukas wouldn't be back until tomorrow. So much for planning a special meal.

'Eleni,' she acknowledged.

'I'm so sorry to have to tell you Loukas was involved in a street accident and has been taken by ambulance to hospital with a gunshot wound. He's currently undergoing emergency surgery. The company's helicopter is on its way to collect you. I'll meet you at the helipad, a car will be waiting at the front entrance and I'll accompany you to the hospital.'

Alesha felt cold, so icily cold it felt as if her body were in shutdown mode, numb, totally without feeling.

'How bad is it?' She knew she breathed, knew she had a heartbeat…because she could feel its thud, loud in the sudden stillness.

'The full extent of damage won't be known until the bullet is removed. The Andreou family have been informed.'

Oh, dear God…what if…? The words banked up and stalled as the horror of what might be filled her vision.

Loukas, injured, bleeding and broken, in surgery attached to numerous machines…

It was almost impossible to believe. The man was invincible.

'I suggest you pack a bag.' Eleni's voice softened a little as she gave the pilot's estimated time of arrival.

'*Kyria?*' Sofia glanced up with a smile as Alesha entered the kitchen…only to have her face sober with concern. 'Something is wrong?'

'I need to go to Athens. It's Loukas.' She managed a brief summation, witnessed the housekeeper's wordless prayer before she turned and moved quickly to the main bedroom.

She banished the overwhelming urge to cry as she thrust a few necessities into a carry-bag. Tears wouldn't achieve a thing, and she had to be strong.

She was unaware of worrying her lip with her teeth, or the faint element of pain.

All she could think of was Loukas. Diminished, filled with painkilling drugs, unconscious, maybe even close to... Dear God, *no*, a silent voice screamed.

He couldn't die. She wouldn't let him.

The agony of never saying she loved him struck her body like a physical pain, and for a moment she couldn't breathe, couldn't move.

What if she didn't have the chance to tell him? What if she was too late?

It seemed an age before she heard the increasing whap-whap sound of incoming rotors, and she watched from the house as the helicopter hovered then lowered down to land.

She was out there in a matter of seconds, climbing up into the cabin, then shutting the door and securing the harness as the pilot increased rotor speed.

The ride seemed to take for ever, and Alesha alighted the instant it was deemed safe to do so, barely remembering to thank the pilot before she moved quickly towards the woman waiting for her.

Presumably she voiced a greeting, but she

retained no memory of having done so as they took the lift down to ground level to where a limousine stood stationary at the entrance.

Traffic snarls lent impatience of a kind she rarely experienced, and if sheer will power aided speed they would have reached the hospital in record time.

Eleni's cellphone beeped and she took the call, speaking rapidly in Greek before cutting the connection.

Alesha demanded, 'That was the hospital?'

'The injury isn't as severe as first thought. The bullet entered his upper left arm and fractured the bone. The surgeon successfully removed the bone fragments and has inserted titanium plates. Loukas is on a drip with pain relief, and he has been transferred to a private suite.'

Alesha was barely aware she traversed a maze of corridors as she demanded details of how, when and why.

'I understand Loukas emerged from the building where he'd attended a meeting and was unable to avoid being caught up in a street demonstration. Police barricaded the area, shots were fired, people arrested. Loukas just happened to be in the wrong place at the wrong time, and one of a few who caught a stray bullet.'

She felt numb as vivid images flashed through her brain, and she automatically followed Eleni as they checked in at a nurses' station before being directed to Loukas' suite.

For a minuscule second she caught an overview of the medical set-up, but it was the man himself who garnered her total attention as her eyes moved hungrily over him, searching his chiselled features, noting a paleness beneath his natural skin colour, his ruffled hair...the sling securing his arm.

Dear heaven.

Another few inches...

Dark eyes held her own, and she felt her body sway beneath the naked emotion evident.

For a moment she couldn't move. She wanted to rush to his side, take his mouth with her own, and say the words she'd held back from gifting him.

'Eleni,' Loukas directed in a quietly voiced drawl. 'You will allow us some privacy, if you please. Stand guard outside the door, and allow no one—' his eyes bore the strength of his command '—I repeat *no one*, to enter this suite until my wife appears in the corridor.'

Within seconds they were alone, and Alesha was powerless to prevent the tears welling in her eyes. Blinking hard did nothing to dispel them, and they spilled over to roll ignominiously down each cheek.

'Come here.'

His voice held a gentleness that almost undid her, and she moved to the side of his bed.

A faint smile curved his lips. 'Closer.'

He lifted a hand and brushed each cheek with the soft pad of his thumb, dispersing the warm moisture that continued to flow unchecked.

'Tears, *agape mou*?' His voice seemed deeper than usual and the slight accent it bore on occasion had become more pronounced.

'I love you.' Saying it seemed more important than anything else.

Just getting the words out released some of the pent-up fear she'd harboured from the moment of Eleni's call. For it had acted as a catalyst, flinging her into the darkness where she was forced to think of her life without him.

Something that acted like a spear through her heart…impossibly painful, unconscionable, *impossible*.

For in that moment, she knew she'd surely die, too.

His gorgeous mouth curved, and her own trembled as he shaped her head and urged it down to within touching distance of his own.

'You think I don't know?' His lips touched her own, sensed the faint quiver and savoured the sweetness.

'*Theos.*' The sound was a soft groan against her mouth. 'I want more of you than this.'

'Not going to happen,' she murmured a trifle

shakily an instant before his tongue swept her mouth, seeking the sensitive tissues, staking a claim.

Evocative and incredibly sensual, she became temporarily lost in the magical chemistry they shared.

For several heart-stopping seconds she had little recognition of time or place…there was just the heat, the solid *live* feel of his mouth on hers, his hands cradling her head.

Soon, much too soon he trailed gentle fingers down her cheek, pressed a thumb-pad to the soft centre of her lower lip, then he released her.

'You're my life,' he vowed gently. 'Everything.'

Her lips trembled at the wealth of emotion flooding her body, and the moisture she'd so recently conquered welled in her eyes.

'Don't cry,' Loukas groaned, and she shook her head.

'I'm not.'

'No?' There was a tinge of humour in his voice as she brushed shaky fingers over each cheek.

'When Eleni rang,' she began, unable to control the way her body trembled, 'it killed me to think you could die without me saying you mean more to me than life itself.' Her eyes held his, beseeching him to understand. 'That without you—' She faltered, and held up a hand, palm outwards, when he sought to pull her close. 'Don't—please. I need to say this.'

Mere words didn't seem to cover what she wanted, *needed* to convey.

'My experience with Seth destroyed any faith I had in men,' she owned with a watery smile. 'Karsouli became my life. Every waking hour was devoted to the family firm. When Dimitri brought up the question of a suitable heir for the next generation, I offered to have a child via a sperm donor and artificial insemination…which he refused to countenance at any cost.'

Her eyes held his, steady, unblinking. 'When I was acquainted with the marriage clause in his will, I wanted to run, but I *lived* for Karsouli, and I refused to give it up, even if it meant I had to marry you.'

She swallowed the sudden lump that rose in her throat.

'I tried to convince myself I could set the terms…to maintain control. Except it didn't work.' She used her teeth to worry her lower lip. 'You were *there*, a constant I steadily accepted. *Wanted* on a level I had difficulty attempting to comprehend.' Her eyes clouded a little. 'I thought I could sleep…have sex with you,' she amended. 'Only to baulk at the last moment.'

Loukas reached out and tucked her hand within his own.

'You were patient, understanding,' Alesha expounded softly. Her fingers threaded through his own. 'And what I imagined was merely sexual chemistry became more. Something so much deeper, I was reluctant to give it the name it deserved.'

'Do you have any idea of my anger when I discovered what your ex had subjected you to?' Loukas queried with dangerous quietness. 'If I could have put my hands on him...' His eyes darkened with barely controlled rage.

She lifted their linked hands and lightly brushed her lips to his knuckles.

'It annihilated me at the time,' she admitted with painful honesty. 'But I survived.' She managed a winsome smile. 'The experience eventually led me to *you*...and the kind of happiness I never thought I would ever find.'

He tugged her in and cupped her nape, brought her head down to his own and took possession of her mouth in a kiss that sent the blood fizzing through her veins.

When at last he released her, she could only look at him with her heart, her love there for him to see.

'*Agape mou*,' he began in a voice husky with emotion. 'You crept beneath my skin, affected me as no other woman did, or ever will, and you invaded my heart, my soul. Until you became the very air I breathe. *You*. Only you.'

Her mouth shook a little, and she struggled to contain the ache of emotional tears. 'You complete me…in every way there is.' She took a moment to find her voice. 'Losing you would be more than I could bear.' She closed her eyes in an effort to still the well of tears threatening to spill…and lost as two overflowed to roll slowly down each cheek. Somehow it no longer mattered if he witnessed her emotional meltdown and she lifted her eyelids without any sense of shame. 'Today I had to face how close it came to being a reality.'

A sound emerged from Loukas' throat as he traced each rivulet and gently dispensed the moisture.

A distinct double-knock sounded, and the door was pushed open to reveal a stern-faced nursing sister who barrelled into the suite.

Alesha failed to comprehend the rapid flow of Greek, but the severe tone was sufficient to convey the nurse's disapproval!

Loukas' silky response did little to appease as the woman checked the saline drip, and took note of his vital signs, then she directed Alesha a stern look before exiting the suite.

'You need to rest,' Alesha said quietly, noting the faint weariness etching his features. He had to be feeling the after-effects of anaesthetic, combined with pain. 'I'll go get some coffee and check back in an hour.'

Loukas' dark eyes seared her own. 'Soon.'

A slight smile curved her lips. 'Rest.' The admonishment held humour, then she turned and walked from the suite, discovered Eleni waiting in the corridor, and by mutual consent they shared coffee.

'The driver is on call and will take you to Loukas' home in Kifissia whenever you're ready to leave the hospital,' Loukas' PA informed her as she handed over a card. 'Just ring this number and he'll wait for you outside the main entrance. I've also added my own number in case you need help of any kind.'

'Thanks.' Alesha's gratitude was genuine as she bade Eleni goodnight.

It wasn't difficult to elicit details regarding Loukas' ongoing treatment, his stay in hospital and the expected length of his recovery.

There was a need to alert the Sydney office the sojourn in Greece would necessarily be extended by at least a week or two…and why.

Loukas was asleep when she re-entered his suite, and she slid quietly into a chair facing his bed, exulting in the opportunity to examine his beloved features unobserved.

Strong facial bone structure, the fine lines bracketing each cheek, more deeply etched in repose. The shaped fullness of his mouth stirred emotions deep inside in memory of how it felt to have him possess her own. A firm jaw, denoting a strength of purpose and a certain ruthlessness.

Integrity, honesty…qualities he possessed in spades.

He was her saviour, her warrior, her protector, her love…everything.

As she was *his*. Mind, body and soul.

No more misgivings or doubts. No more pretending to hide beneath a veil of indifference or pretence.

The important factor, the major one…he *cared*.

The world suddenly became a brighter place as she hugged the knowledge close.

'Alesha,' a soft masculine voice drawled with amusement, and she sent him a stunningly sweet smile.

'Hi.'

'Where were you? Sydney?' Loukas teased. 'The island?'

'Here,' she said simply. 'Just looking at you.'

He patted the bed. 'You're too far away.'

'And incur the nurse's wrath again?'

Her eyes held a wicked gleam that did little to still the heat flooding his groin. 'Minx.' The edges of his mouth formed a wry smile. 'Enjoy your feeling of power, hmm?'

A soft laugh emerged from her lips. 'I am, believe me.'

'Not for long.' The promise was there, vibrantly alive and tantalising. He watched her eyes coalesce and become dark with a sense of satisfaction. 'Count on it,' he added gently.

'I doubt you'll be…' she paused delicately '…able to manage the kind of physical activity you have in mind for a while.'

One eyebrow rose in quizzical disbelief. 'You think not?'

'Feasible,' she allowed. 'If I do all the work.'

'*Agape mou*,' Loukas drawled, 'that's the plan.'

She pretended to give it consideration. 'I don't think the hospital staff would be impressed.'

'You realize I can discharge myself and employ the services of a nurse?'

Alesha deliberately widened her eyes. 'Why, when you have excellent medical attention here twenty-four/seven?'

He waited a beat. 'I need to hold you through the night.' His voice held a gentleness that almost undid her. 'Be there when you wake.'

Her heart yearned to be there with him, cradled close to his side…safe, secure, *loved* as she'd given up hope of being loved, for herself, not as Alesha Karsouli, the favoured daughter of Dimitri Karsouli.

The door swung open to admit a nurse bearing

medication. Loukas took it without argument and bore the routine of recorded notations, and accepted the stern dictum that visiting hours were over.

Any privacy was limited, and Alesha crossed to his side, brushed his mouth with her own…or at least that was her intention, except he curved a hand round her nape and held her there for countless seconds as he deepened the kiss before reluctantly releasing her.

He noted the pink colouring her cheeks and smiled. 'Sleep well, *yineka mou.*'

The driver was waiting for her in the entry lounge, and he escorted her to the car, saw her seated, then he negotiated traffic as he headed to Loukas' Kifissia mansion where Hera greeted her and made anxious enquiries about Loukas' injuries.

'You have eaten, *kyria*?'

She hadn't, at least not in quite a while, and she gratefully accepted the offer of a light meal before heading upstairs to shower and change.

It was late when she retired for the night, and she read for a while before extinguishing the light.

Sleep should have come easily, except she lay awake addressing events of the day…visualizing in her mind the street demonstration and how a bullet had almost cost her the man she'd learnt to love more than life itself.

Imagining how it went down, the ambulance with its medical team attempting to stem the blood flow, assessing Loukas' injuries, the emergency dash to hospital, the surgery…and the relief on learning he was going to be fine, when she'd feared the worst.

Somehow the scenario slid into her subconscious mind and emerged in a nightmare so dark, so vivid, she woke with tears streaming down her cheeks and his name on her lips.

There was a pressing need to replace that image with another, and she retreated to the en suite to press a cool flannel to her face before collecting an electronic reader from her bag. Then she slid into bed, bunched a few pillows behind her back and settled in to read.

Alesha ate a light breakfast and planned the day around hospital visits…with emphasis on the need to keep busy. A shopping expedition, perhaps, with a view to purchasing a few items to gift friends on her return to Sydney? The gorgeous pendant she'd seen displayed in a shop window would be perfect for Lacey…if only she could remember *which* shop and *where* in the city.

She'd ask Cristos to accompany her, and with luck they'd be able to locate it.

Athens held a tremendous sense of history,

with aged buildings that held an aura of ancient times and warriors of old. Open-air food and craft markets blended with modern department stores, galleries, and individual stores.

'Monastiráki and Pláka,' Cristos informed as he sought parking prior to midday.

While strolling the Pláka she visited Lexi's studio and purchased the bracelet she'd admired and matching ear-studs with a view to gifting it to Lacey for Christmas.

Thirty minutes in, Alesha recognized the window display with its dazzling items, and Cristos' mention of the name Andreou resulted in the manager insisting on a private showing.

'Apparently you possess a certain reputation for purchasing expensive gifts,' she teased Loukas later in the day, and saw the edges of his mouth lift with cynical amusement.

'It bothers you?'

He had a past that included any number of women. She'd seen the tabloids over the years...slender beautiful women captured by camera clinging to his arm at one function or another.

'Should it?'

Loukas' eyes darkened as he took in her carefully composed features, her steady gaze, and sensed the faint indecision beneath her query.

'No.' She had to know there could never be
any other woman for him…only her. She was the
light of his life. *Theos*. All of it, the very air he
breathed. Without her, he'd lose the will to live.

For a brief moment he silently damned being
confined.

He wanted out of here, away from hospital
routine and its restrictions. Most of all, he wanted
her…

When it came time for her to leave he kissed
her so deeply her eyes widened with momentary
surprise.

Intense passion, leashed…and primitive
beneath the surface.

Just to look at him made her toes curl…not to
mention other parts of her body.

She lifted a hand and placed the palm over his
cheek as her mouth formed a tremulous smile.
'Take care.'

Then she turned and walked from the suite,
paused at Reception to text Cristos she was ready
to leave the hospital.

'Where would you like to go, *kyria*?'

She'd done the shopping thing, and didn't feel
inclined to wander the boutiques without a purpose.

Loukas' palatial home beckoned. She'd visit
the kitchen, make a cup of tea and filch a snack
from the refrigerator.

'Kifissia, Cristos.'

The beautiful mansion seemed large with its high ceilings, marble floors and solid furniture. Alesha's footsteps echoed as she crossed the foyer and ascended the curved staircase to the upper level.

On reaching the master suite, she toed off her stilettos, then she discarded her outer clothes and pulled on comfortable leggings and a loose-knit top whose hemline rested low on her thighs.

Tea, she decided, and chose to forgo the snack. The last day or two had wrought a change in her desire for food, and she sipped her tea, then checked her watch, calculated the time in Sydney and reached for her cellphone, hit Lacey's number on speed dial and heard her friend pick up.

'Alesha! How are you? *Where* are you? What's happening?'

It was easy to laugh, wonderful to talk, and great to catch up as they exchanged mutual news.

Ten minutes, fifteen…Alesha wasn't sure when a slight sound alerted her attention, and she paused mid-sentence as Loukas entered the room.

Startled disbelief widened her eyes as the words fell from her lips without thought. 'What are you doing here?'

'Alesha?' Lacey demanded over the phone. 'Is everything okay?'

'I—Yes.' Distracted didn't begin to describe it. 'You should be in hospital.'

'Loukas is home?'

Conducting a three-way conversation when attempting to collect one's wits was bound to be…disjointed, to say the least.

'Lacey?' Loukas queried, and when she nodded he took the phone from her hand. 'Alesha will call you tomorrow. And, yes, thank you. I'm fine. Take care.'

With that he disconnected the call, tossed the phone onto the sofa, then he caught hold of her hand and drew her to her feet.

'You shouldn't—'

'Later,' he said gently.

She opened her mouth, and closed it again as he slid a hand beneath the weight of her hair to cup her nape, then he lowered his head and kissed her with a thoroughness that left her faintly breathless.

'And that was…because?'

'You need to ask?'

A delicious smile curved her lips. 'Uh-huh.'

'Minx.'

He felt so good. To think—

A hand caught her chin and tilted it. 'Don't.'

So many emotions…an entire gamut ranging from fear to relief.

And joy. True happiness.

Loukas had gifted her both.

Love. The most precious gift of all.

Alesha wanted to cry…and laugh…but most of all she needed to offer her touch and savour his own.

To celebrate *life*. Theirs, together…for all time.

The words would come later.

But first, she determined to tease him a little.

'Discharging yourself against medical advice isn't a wise decision. And don't think you're going to discard that arm-sling any time soon,' she admonished.

His eyes gleamed, dark, liquid, and incredibly sensual. 'No? I'm sure with care we can work around it.'

She tried for stern remonstrance, and failed miserably. 'You should rest.'

'I plan to. In bed. With you.'

'The emphasis will be *rest*.'

A warm smile curved his generous mouth. 'Eventually.'

'Have you eaten?'

'You want to talk *food*?'

'I'm thinking of your stamina level,' she managed with a straight face, and felt her nerve-ends curl at the sound of his husky laughter.

His hand slid beneath her top and sought the

warm skin, murmuring his appreciation at her lack of a bra, and her body arched into his as he palmed each breast in turn, creating a delicate friction on each tender peak.

A sigh of pleasure escaped from her lips seconds before his mouth closed over hers, and she became lost in the emotional tide he created.

Together they moved upstairs to their suite, undressed each other slowly, she helping him with such gentle care it brought him undone.

Together they savoured each lingering touch... the slide of a hand, the trail of gentle fingers. Lips seeking and caressing sensitive pulse-points, vulnerable hollows.

Lovemaking in its most sensual form, Alesha accorded as Loukas lay down on the bed, and she moved over him, taking her time to explore him gently with her mouth...finessing each light touch until he groaned and urged possession.

She slid down onto him with care, and her eyes didn't leave his as she began to move with captivating sensuality, exulting in the control, the power as she set the pace.

He growled deep in his throat when she lowered her head and brushed the length of her hair back and forth across his chest, then began tormenting him with her lips as she leaned in and inched her way up to the hollow at the base of his throat, traced it with the tip of her tongue before seeking his mouth in an erotic kiss.

Afterwards she lay curled close against him, her head pillowed into the curve of his shoulder as his hand drifted a soothing pattern over her hip, lingered there, then travelled to settle at her nape.

It was late when they rose, showered together as Alesha encased his injured arm in waterproof plastic, towelled him dry, then helped him into a robe before tending to herself as he re-entered the bedroom.

When she emerged, he handed her a slim jeweller's box. 'I have something for you.' The warmth of his smile melted her heart. 'Open it.'

An exquisite diamond necklace lay nestled against a bed of black velvet. Brilliant pink Argyle stones alternated with blue fire in a delicate setting that showcased a beautiful pear-drop pendant. A matching bracelet and ear-studs completed the set.

'It's beautiful.'

It was the one she'd admired displayed in a jeweller's window. Cristos must have mentioned her interest…coincidence didn't stretch so far.

'Thank you.' She swallowed the sudden lump that rose in her throat as she became lost in the gleaming darkness of his eyes. 'But you've already given me the most precious gift of all.' Her eyes misted, and she blinked hard to dispense the moisture. 'You. Just you.' Her breath hitched as she sought control of her emotions. 'Nothing else compares.'

With one exception, Loukas added silently. The fitting conclusion of measures he'd put in place to deprive her ex of every last cent he'd gained from Alesha's ill-fated short-lived marriage. To date, the bank had foreclosed on Seth's home. The Porsche he revered had been sold. It was only a matter of time before he'd be forced to walk away from his business.

Several days later the helicopter flew them to the island where the gentle ebb and flow of the water against the sandy cove lent an air of tranquillity.

The days were pleasant with cool temperatures and rain overnight, but they didn't care. For it was there they spent an idyllic few days, made leisurely love, taking time when the rain cleared to wander the beach, pausing every now and then to examine a piece of driftwood, a smooth pebble, to the sound of a keening gull, the excited bark of the golden retriever who called the island home.

Soon, they'd return to the mainland, and within days board a flight to Sydney, where life would settle into its former routine.

With possibly one exception, and she hugged the knowledge close, not wanting to share until the tiny life she was instinctively sure she nurtured could be confirmed.

On the final day they pulled on boots, donned jackets, and took the dog for a late afternoon walk. A breeze caught the length of Alesha's hair and tossed it into a tumbled mess, and after attempting to confine it she simply laughed and gave up, pausing to look out over the choppy sea.

Loukas stepped behind her and wrapped an arm around her slender waist, then he rested his chin against the top of her head.

Only that morning he'd received the confirmation his strategy with Alesha's ex had reached its completion.

Seth Armitage's investments had diminished to almost nil; he'd been forced to sell all his assets at rock-bottom prices, and his reputation was in tatters. A fitting end for an unscrupulous and cruel man.

It had taken considerable effort to achieve such an outcome, and all the relevant strings were tied…with one exception.

With care he turned her round to face him and extracted a sealed envelope from the pocket of his jacket. 'For you.'

Alesha's eyes widened as she searched his features…and gleaned little other than the deep passion evident, together with something indefinable. Resolve?

'I have everything I need,' Alesha assured quietly.

'Open it.'

She did, releasing the flap with care, and extracting a slim piece of paper. Her lips parted in startled surprise as she identified a certified bank cheque for five million dollars.

Her eyes flew to his. 'What is this?'

'The settlement your father paid your ex for an uncontested divorce on the condition he got out of your life.'

Ohmigod. Her breathing became ragged as shock encompassed her body. *That much?*

'I won't accept it from you,' she refused in a voice husky with emotion.

'It represents the sale of Seth Armitage's business, his home and everything he owned.'

Blood money.

The realization hit her, and she simply looked at him, her eyes locked with his own.

'You ruined him.'

'You doubt I could?'

There was only one answer. 'No.'

He had the power, the ruthlessness to tear Seth limb from figurative limb in a manner that would hurt more than anything else…stripping her ex of everything he'd gained out of their marriage and the divorce.

Loukas captured her chin and tilted it. 'I wanted to kill him for what he did to you.' He traced gentle fingers over her trembling mouth.

'Instead you devised a fitting revenge.'

'One he deserved.'

She was silent for several long minutes as she mustered the courage to reveal details she hadn't told a living soul.

'It began a few days after the wedding,' she began quietly. 'The belittlement when I failed to satisfy him. The cruel taunts when I refused to comply with his demand for kinky sex. I was too uptight, too straight-laced and needed to be taught a lesson.' Her eyes didn't leave his, and she glimpsed his pain, the darkness of his anger…and she placed a soothing hand on his rigid jaw. 'I ended up in hospital with a few fractured ribs, a fractured arm, and bruising.'

She'd started this…she needed to finish it.

'I called a lawyer, and hired security to stand guard in shifts outside my room.'

'Dimitri—'

'Was in Melbourne on business, and was only apprised of my injuries on his return.'

A muscle tensed at the edge of his jaw as he recalled her fear, the nightmares, the evidence of broken and fractured bones.

'Yet you didn't press charges.'

'My decision. I didn't want the episode to become fodder for the media or dragged through the court.' She drew a deep breath. 'It was done… over. Seth took a financial settlement.' Her eyes hardened at the amount her father had added to ensure Seth never made any further demand on her again. 'And I moved on with my life.'

'Alesha—'

Anything else he might have said remained stilled as she placed light fingers over his mouth.

'Don't…please.' Her expression softened, her incredible eyes became luminous with emotion. 'We have the future together, *love*…the once-in-a-lifetime kind. Infinitely special,' she added gently. 'Everything I ever wanted…and more, so much more. With you. I can't keep this money, Loukas. I don't want it—it's tainted. But I can put it to some use and help others who might be in the same position as I was—do you agree?'

Loukas lowered his head down to hers and brushed his lips to her forehead.

'I thought the marriage clause in Dimitri's will a cruel and heartless act.' She moved her head to look at him. 'Instead ultimately it became a unique gift.'

'Without question.'

'It would be wonderful if somehow he knows,' she pondered a trifle pensively.

'Perhaps he does.'

She turned slightly and looked out over the bay whose surface rippled beneath the stiffening breeze.

'This is an incredible place,' Alesha voiced wistfully.

His arm tightened a little and she felt his lips nuzzle the sensitive pulse beneath an ear lobe. 'A private haven with no tourists, no marina housing a host of boats.'

Just us…heaven.

'I want to thank you,' she began quietly.

'For what, in particular?'

He sounded mildly amused, and Alesha smiled a little.

'Believing in me,' she said simply. 'Being there. You're my life. My love. Everything.'

Loukas turned her to face him, and she became lost in the wealth of emotion evident in his dark eyes.

He brushed his lips across her own, parted them, then lingered to savour a little. 'I imagined a contented union, a compliant wife, cementing a successful business merger.'

'Instead you gained a neurotic divorcee with emotional baggage.'

He drew her lower lip between his teeth and nipped the fullness. 'A beautiful young woman,' he corrected, 'who crept beneath my skin and captured my heart.' He eased the tip of his tongue over her lip, soothing it.

'You taught me to believe in love,' Alesha added gently.

'*Agape mou.* I exist only for you.'

She wanted to cry…and almost did. He was a very special man. She intended to show him just how special every day for the rest of her life.

Her eyes acquired a wicked sparkle as she tilted her head to one side and regarded him with musing humour. 'The sex helped. You're rather good at it.'

A husky laugh emerged from his throat as he caught hold of her hand and threaded his fingers through her own. 'Let's go back to the house.'

The air held a chill as they trod the path and traversed the slight incline. The house was warm, and she turned towards the kitchen.

'It's Sofia's night off. I'll fix dinner.'

'Later.' He pulled her close and took her mouth in a deep slow kiss, then he captured her hand and led her upstairs to the bedroom.

EPILOGUE

A YEAR later a number of invited guests, including Constantine, Angelina, Daria and Lexi who flew in from Athens, attended a party at Loukas and Alesha's Point Piper mansion to celebrate the christening of their twins…Sebastian Loukas and his sister Sienna Lucille.

Two beautiful children whose birth via Caesarean section saw Sienna emerge seconds ahead of her brother, and whose cry…*howl*, her father amended…was loud in protest. Not to be outdone, Sebastian surpassed her in pitch, and only subsided when he was placed into his mother's arms.

Now three months of age, they slept in their nursery in adjacent cribs, in the care of a nanny.

'You have gifted us the joy of beautiful grandchildren,' Constantine declared as he and Angelina prepared to leave the party at evening's end.

'Beautiful,' Daria echoed, and brushed her lips

to Alesha's cheek, before she turned to Loukas. 'You're a fortunate man.' She assumed a stern expression, which was totally contrived. 'Take good care of your family.'

'With my life, *Thia*,' he assured gently.

It was late when Loukas set the security system after the last guest departed, and he curved an arm around Alesha's waist as they crossed the foyer.

Together they ascended the stairs and crossed to the nursery. A dimmed night light revealed two dark-haired babes, their chubby faces serene in sleep.

'Special,' Loukas said softly. 'So very special, *agape mou*.'

They moved quietly from the room and entered their bedroom suite.

'Have I told you how much I adore you?' Loukas turned her into his arms and took possession of her mouth in a kiss that stole the breath from her throat.

Only every night. 'A wife can't hear too much of a good thing,' she responded with teasing lightness, knowing every word came from the heart.

Her pregnancy had delighted him, for he'd been there for her every step of the way, loving the changes to her body, amazed at the discovery the babe she carried was in fact *two*. He'd gowned up and witnessed their birth, marvelled at the miracle, and become as much of a hands-on father as time would allow.

'I've been thinking.'

'Why do I suddenly have the feeling that could be dangerous?'

Her mouth curved into a winsome smile. 'This is a very large home with several bedrooms.'

His eyes darkened measurably. 'You say this…because?'

'Perhaps we should consider providing Sebastian and Sienna with a brother or sister.'

'Are you sure you're ready for another pregnancy so soon?'

'How does May sound to you?'

'A year from now?'

'Ah, my husband is good at maths.'

'Witch.'

'It will give you time to get used to the idea,' Alesha said with a wicked gleam as she linked her hands at his nape.

'My concern is only for you.'

'I know.'

And she did, aware she'd come full circle in a marriage to a man she hadn't expected to love more than life itself.

LARGER-PRINT BOOKS!

GET 2 FREE LARGER-PRINT NOVELS PLUS 2 FREE GIFTS!

PASSION GUARANTEED SEDUCTION

HPLP10R

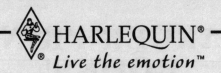

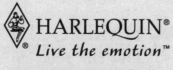

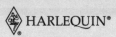

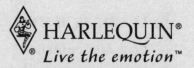

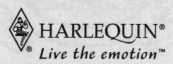

Harlequin® Historical
Historical Romantic Adventure!

Imagine a time of chivalrous knights and unconventional ladies, roguish rakes and impetuous heiresses, rugged cowboys and spirited frontierswomen—these rich and vivid tales will capture your imagination!

Harlequin Historical . . . they're too good to miss!

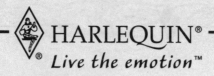

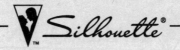